About the author

Art Lester grew up in a southern American environment rich in stories. His godfather was the grandson of Joel Chandler Harris, author of the Uncle Remus tales. He was fortunate as a child in having access to African-American storytellers, whose repertoire was built on stories brought by slaves from their African origins. In later life, he got training in storytelling from Ewan MacColl, the folk singer/songwriter and stage director.

For the past twenty-five years he has served as a Unitarian minister to congregations in London and Dublin. He is the author of the award-winning Seeing with Your Ears and five other books.

He shares his time in London and in a small village of the Sierra Nevada in Southern Spain with his wife, Gilly Fraser, a TV scriptwriter and playwright.

The Truth In 60 Seconds

Art Lester

Copyright © 2016 Art Lester

All rights reserved, including the right to reproduce this book, or portions thereof in any form. No part of this text may be reproduced, transmitted, downloaded, decompiled, reverse engineered, or stored, in any form or introduced into any information storage and retrieval system, in any form or by any means, whether electronic or mechanical without the express written permission of the author.

ISBN: 978-1-326-73632-3

PublishNation,
www.publishnation.co.uk

THE TRUTH IN 60 SECONDS

Dim Lantern Books
London

Text © Art Lester 2016

Drawings © Steven Appleby 2016

THE TRUTH IN 60 SECONDS

99 TALES TO SET YOUR INNER CLOCK BY

Art Lester

Illuminated by Steven Appleby

Some Tales to Set your Inner Clock By

A picture may be worth a thousand words, but a good story—one told over and over—must be worth a million. Stories are the way wisdom has been transmitted from generation to generation since the time when the first pictures were appearing on cave walls. Stories are not just the result of acquiring language; they may be the reason language became necessary.

The parables of Jesus, Aesop and the Hassidim merge seamlessly with the forehead-slapping punchlines of Zen stories and the oblique but penetrating humour of Mullah Nasruddin, the Sufi wise fool. Fast forward to the Uncle Remus tales, the Brothers Grimm and the tall tales of Mark Twain. Eavesdrop on countless bedtimes in innumerable children's bedrooms, and you begin to see just how important the good story, well told, can be.

Half of the 99 stories in The Truth in Sixty Seconds are re-told traditional stories from many sources, and the other half are recently discovered. I say discovered instead of invented, because I feel that really good stories, "true" ones, exist outside of the usual boundaries of time and culture. You just have to go looking for them.

Art Lester

Contents

Once upon a Time They Lived Happily ever After	13
The Eternal Flame	15
Do God a Favour	17
Proof of Faith	21
Guarding the Rock of Truth	23
The Circle of Grapes	25
The Magical Vessel	27
No Vacancy in Heaven	31
The Missing Half Hour	34
The Churn	37
On Your Bike	39
The Well-Trained Ass	40
The Dimmest Lantern	43
The Gift of the Sky	47
The Last Words	51
You're Welcome	54
The Teacher of Jade	57
Shrinking Monsters	60
I Have Not Yet Sold My Shop	62
The Cries of the Poor	65
How to Make Pots	67
Alchemy	69
Give Everything	72
The Wrong Fox	74
The Peach Seed Necklace	76

Dishing the Dirt	81
Less is More	84
The Dirtiest Face	86
Spooning Out the Lake	88
The Doctor of Unicorns	90
Poverty is Expensive	93
The Seeker's Dilemma	96
The Horse Might Talk	98
Survival of the Fittest	100
I'm Out Here	106
Two Ways to Become Rich	108
The Tiger's Whisker	111
The Seeds	118
The Parrot Who Made it Rain	120
Turning Wine into Water	122
The Most Dangerous Animal	124
How not to be a Farmer	127
The Strongest Trap	131
The Locksmith's Escape	133
The Spiritual Aspirant	135
The Singing Creek	137
The Secret of Happiness	142
How to make it Rain	143
The Prophet's Rock	147
Truth, One Penny	149

X Marks the Spot	152
The Voice of the Soul	156
Why White Folks are White	159
Where Money Grows on Trees	161
What is Goodness?	163
The Most Spiritual Music	165
The Meanest Man in the World	167
The Greatest Gardener	169
The Burning Question	173
Stop, Thief!	175
In Disguise	180
All the Names of God	181
God in a Box	183
A Difficult Beggar	185
Farming Wild Boars	190
Heavenly Pie	192
The Magic Lens	195
The House of Spots	198
The Inescapable Cell	201
The Light Bringer	203
The Man Who would be Rich	205
The Magic Ribbon	210
What Noise?	212
You have Saved Yourself	216
The Master of the Rags	219
Ripples	223
99	225

The Broken Jug	229
Dinnertime in Heaven	231
A Donkey for a Cat	234
Giving Up Gambling	236
Krishna's Chess Game	237
Heed Your Dream	240
Seven Fish	247
The Castaway	249
The Chipped Cup	251
The Object of Worship	255
The Rooster Prince	258
The Speech	262
The Writing Lesson	264
Un-chopping a Walnut Tree	266

FOR KIDS:

The White Fat Little Dog	269
Too Generous	273
The Millionaires' Club	276
How to Make a Million Pounds	284
Dozy Rosie	286
Won't Power	290
Don't Think about a Bear	293
The Day God Popped Round	297

Once Upon a Time
They Lived Happily Ever After

The trusted advisor and companion of the king had recently died. Along with his sorrow at losing such an old friend, he was concerned that there would be no one among the ranks of minor courtiers who could replace him. He thought long and hard, and then decided to test the wisdom of several who might qualify: two old-timers who had been around for many years agreeing with the king's every word, and one young man who, until recently, had been a tutor to the children of the court.

To do this, he announced that he was going to make a state visit to a neighbouring kingdom to visit his cousin. He invited one of the old retainers to join him on the journey. After they had set out in his carriage, he said to the would-be advisor, "Shorten the journey for me, please."

Believing that the king wanted him to demonstrate his knowledge of the roads of the kingdom, the advisor ordered the driver to weave through a series of short-cuts, some of which were overgrown with branches and rutted through disuse. The king sighed.

"Turn back," he said.

Arriving back at the palace with the dumbfounded courtier, the king asked the second candidate to join him in the carriage. After a few miles, he said once again, "Please shorten the journey for me." The second courtier leapt onto the front of the carriage, pushed the driver aside and began whipping the horses to gain more speed. The carriage bounced and jolted dangerously along the road until the king shouted, "Stop! Return to the palace immediately!"

Back at the palace, the king dismissed the second courtier and asked the new young man to join him. After a while, the king said for the third time, "Please shorten the journey for me." The former tutor sat quietly for a moment, and then said, "Once upon a time…" He told a story that so engrossed the king with its twists and turns and hidden meanings that the journey seemed to take no time at all.

Upon returning from his state visit, the young man was appointed the king's most trusted advisor and, naturally, lived happily ever after.

Based on a story told by Rev Bill Darlison
in "The Shortest Distance".

The Eternal Flame

The cave in the high mountain had been the dwelling of holy men for centuries. As one grew old, another came to sit in his place, guarding a flame in a simple clay lamp that had never been extinguished.

Pilgrims came to sit silently by the sage, who was usually rapt in prayer. They brought gifts of rice and tea and oil for the lamp. Some came with problems, others with illnesses. The master offered no advice, but people felt they benefitted from simply being in his presence.

One day a merchant came, leading his small son by the hand. He had come in hope that the calming presence of the master would help the mischievous boy, who had already been excluded from school by the time he was eight. The boy squirmed and complained as he was made to sit cross-legged with his father near the silent master.

Without warning, the boy jumped to his feet, ran forward, and in front of the horrified gaze of the other pilgrims, blew out the lamp. There was a collective gasp from the group. The master opened his eyes, looked at the lamp, now growing cold, and then at the boy, who was still running in circles.

He rose to his feet. Everyone could see that he was about to speak. Still shocked, they waited as the master raised one finger in the air, and said:

"Has anyone got a match?"

Do God a Favour

The old man had grown very rich, by spending very little and always keeping a sharp eye out for any opportunity to profit. He owned houses in three towns and was notorious for evicting tenants at the first sign of insolvency. Since he was too busy making money, he never married, and as he grew old, saw fewer and fewer people.

For some months he had been feeling that his life was nearing its end. He wanted to turn his same sharp eye on his prospects for getting into heaven and guaranteeing himself a place by whatever means. Too weak to travel, he sent for a certain holy man who, it was rumoured, spoke often to God himself.

When the holy man came at last, the old man was confined to his bed. He asked the sage to stand at the foot of the bed in the light of the window, in order to see him clearly.

"I am old now," he began.

"Yes, I can see that," said the holy man, who was dressed

in rough ordinary clothing like a workman.

"I shall soon die, and I want to be sure I am going to heaven."

"Hmmmm. Yes, I see," said the sage brightly.

"What must I pay you to intervene for me with God?"

The sage looked at his hands for a moment, as if calculating a sum.

"Have you given regular alms to the poor?" he asked suddenly.

"No. What has that to do with it?" growled the old man. "I believe God helps those who help themselves. I have always helped myself, and now look at the fine house I live in."

"And your tenants," said the holy man, as if he had not heard. "Have you been generous with them?"

"I have been fair and always within the law," snapped the old man crossly.

The sage seemed to be thinking. "I will go away and have a word with God tonight," he said at last. "I will return tomorrow with the price you must pay for admission to heaven."

The old man sighed and closed his eyes. He was unused to being asked to wait.

The following day the holy man was back. He seemed very chipper. "Good news," he said.

"You have spoken with God?" asked the invalid.

"Yes. He said He was very pleased to guarantee your admission to heaven, provided you are willing to do Him a favour."

"A favour? An expensive favour?"

"No, not at all. That is the good news. He simply asks you to bring something with you to the heavenly gates."

"What?" asked the old man suspiciously.

"Do you remember Hassan, the tailor? He was a very pious man, always very generous to the poor and always remembered them in his prayers."

"Yes, of course. He is dead now, I believe."

"Yes, he's in heaven with God, but his one wish, even among the glories of the heavenly kingdom, is to do something for God. He longs to sew Him a new robe, since the old one has lasted a million years."

"And..?"

"Unfortunately, he lacks a needle with which to sew the cloak. God wishes to know if you would be willing to bring one along when you die."

"A needle? Nothing more?"

"No, just that."

"And he guarantees that I will have a place in heaven?"

"Yes," said the holy man, smiling.

"Done!" said the old man. For a moment he felt almost as if his strength had returned. He loved driving a hard bargain, and how much sweeter it was to win a bargain from God!

After the holy man had gone, the old man sent his servant to the market to buy a needle. "An ordinary one will do," he cautioned. "No point in being excessive."

He lay back and planned his trip to heaven. But then a

thought occurred to him. Where would he carry the needle? Ah, he thought, I know. I will pin it to my grave sheets. He relaxed again.

He awoke from sleep a few minutes later with a bothersome thought. Why, the grave clothes would surely rot away, so the needle would be lost. He thought hard. I know, he thought at last, I will have it placed in my mouth, so that it stays with me. But then a second thought occurred suddenly on its heels. My mouth, too will decompose in the grave, and I would not have the needle.

He fumed and sent for the holy man again. When he arrived the old man spoke crossly. "I have been tricked, haven't I? Unless you can tell me how to carry the needle to heaven, I will not be able to fulfil my end of the bargain.

The holy man sighed, and spread his hands. "I fear I cannot help you there," he said.

"The fact is, nothing earthly can be carried to heaven, can it?"

The sage stood quietly, watching the old man's face. He knew he was seeing someone change before his eyes.

"Then what of my great wealth?" the old man said, as if to himself.

Thereafter the poor of the village were less poor, and the tailor Hassan's new cloak was unnecessary.

Proof of Faith

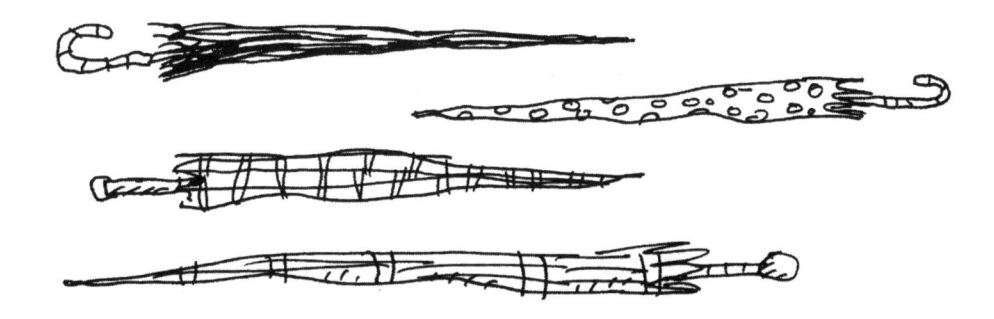

A long and devastating drought had afflicted the village, and people had become desperate. Food became scarce and what little there was, was very expensive. The elders gathered and discussed the problem. After a lot of complaining with very little in the way of ideas, a man stood up and said that he had heard of a holy man who was able to make it rain.

"We're desperate enough to try anything," the headman said. "Summon the holy man and let's give it a try."

Messages were sent, and at the next meeting of the council, the man reported that the holy man was willing to come, but had one requirement.

"He said that God will only comply with our request if someone from this village has faith in Him. He cannot do it alone."

"Tell him we are all people of faith here. Let him come," the headman said.

The following day a small man with a large bundle on his back appeared in the village. He asked that everyone assemble in the square to beseech God for rain.

The crowds began to gather, and by late afternoon everyone was there. Farmers had left their dry fields, wives had left their bare kitchens and even the children had stopped playing their games. The holy man stood in the centre of the square and looked carefully at everyone. He walked through the masses, apparently looking for something among them. After scrutinising everyone, he stood on a box and addressed the crowd.

"I have come under the belief that this village was populated by people of faith. I see that it is not true, however, and so it is pointless to ask God for rain." He turned and walked away from the stunned assembly, still carrying his bulky burden.

The headman hurried after him and caught his arm.

"Master," he said, "Why have you decided we are not people of faith?"

The holy man kept walking. Over his shoulder he said, "No one brought an umbrella."

Guarding the Rock of Truth

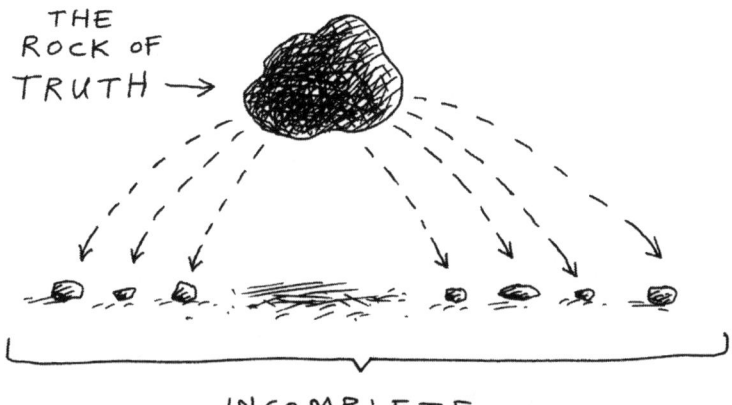

```
THE
ROCK OF
TRUTH →
```

(diagram: The Rock of Truth at top with dashed arrows radiating down to small rock fragments below, labeled:)

INCOMPLETE FRAGMENTS OF TRUTH

The Guardian of the Rock of Truth was entertaining his grandson on the mountain top. After several millennia he felt the need of a little company, and it wouldn't hurt the lad to learn a few things about what Grandpa did all day. They sat and watched as various humans below attempted to scale the mountain where the large Rock gleamed in the sunlight. They watched them as they got side-tracked or discouraged. Sometimes people actually fell in their attempts.

"Why do you need to guard the Rock, Grandpa?" asked the boy.

"Because the truth is dangerous to humans."

"Why is that?"

"I'll explain another time," said the Guardian. He was looking closely at a human who was getting very near the summit. They watched as a man scaled the last few feet of the climb and stood unsteadily blinking in the sun.

The Guardian walked over and stood between the ragged and exhausted man and the Rock. "I'm afraid you can't go any further," he said.

"But I want the truth," complained the man.

"Sorry. Out of the question," said the Guardian.

He turned back toward his grandson, and the man dashed forward. In a second he had picked up a small piece of the Rock and jumped back onto the trail. The Guardian watched him head down with a sigh.

"Another poor fellow," he said.

"But, Grandpa, he looked happy!" said the boy.

They looked down at the man. He was holding the tiny piece of the Rock of Truth over his head, a look of ecstasy on his face. Far below him they could see a crowd of cheering people who watched as the man made his way down the mountain. The Guardian clucked his tongue and shook his head sadly.

"Are you afraid he will fall, Grandpa? Is that why it's bad for him to have a piece of the truth?"

"No," answered the old man.

"Is it because it will make him ill?"

"No," said the Guardian.

"Then why?" asked the boy impatiently.

"Because now he will take that small piece and start another religion," the Guardian said.

The Circle of Grapes

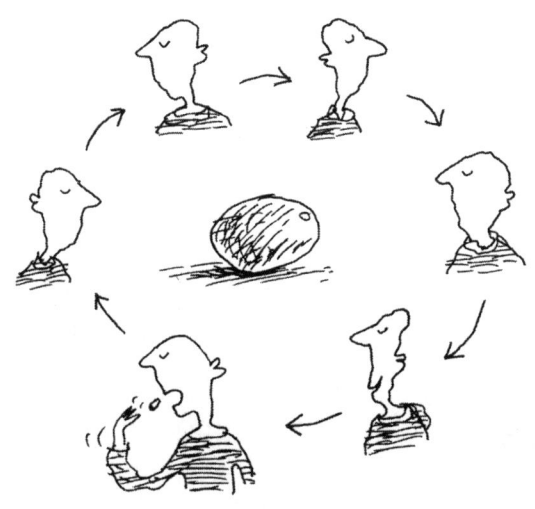

A poor peasant knocked on the big wooden door of a monastery. He was greeted, as always, by a small monk with a smiling face. The peasant reached into his basket and handed the monk a big, beautiful bunch of grapes.

"They're wonderful," said the small monk. "I'm sure the abbot will enjoy them."

"They're not for the abbot," said the peasant. "They're for you."

"For me? Why?" asked the monk.

"Because during all the drought and trouble of the last year you always opened the door for me with a smile. Now the crops have succeeded, and I'd like to reward you."

Thanking him, the monk took the grapes to his cell and stared at them. "They are too good and rich a gift for me," he thought. "I know—Brother Thomas is ill in the infirmary. I'll give them to him to cheer him to recovery."

Brother Thomas was all smiles when he received his gift and thanked the monk profusely. But after he had left, he began to think. He felt that he should find some way to reward the kindness of the apothecary who had tended him through his long illness, and so he gave them to him at the first opportunity.

The apothecary was delighted with his gift, and then gave them to the Abbot, who above all deserved such a fine gift. The Abbot thanked the apothecary, and as soon as he had left, decided to give them to a young novice, whose air of charity had impressed him. He called for the young man and gave him the grapes.

The young novice was overwhelmed by the Abbot's generosity. The grapes were so large and beautiful. He thought of the poor who lived in the nearby village, and made up his mind to find a deserving person to have a sudden unexpected gift.

The peasant who had given the grapes to the gatekeeper was surprised when he looked up from his plough and saw the young novice standing there.

"I thought these grapes might make you happy," said the novice.

"Where did they come from?" asked the peasant, smiling.

"Why from God, of course," said the novice.

"Tell Him I said thanks," said the peasant, and popped a grape into his mouth.

The Magical Vessel

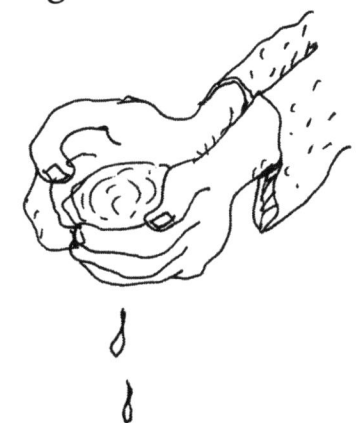

A young farmer had married the woman of his dreams, a delicate, soft-eyed beauty that had been sought by all the young men of his village. She was from a place two days' journey away, across a range of mountains, but the suitors had travelled the roads constantly to see her until her parents agreed to give him her hand.

But soon after the wedding feast was over, the young wife's health began to fail. She grew pale and quiet, and finally began to refuse her food. Doctors were summoned, but none could identify the source of the illness. At last, in desperation, the farmer sent for a wise man who lived in a small hut high in the mountains. He came at dusk one afternoon, a small man in a worn coat, carrying nothing but a staff.

The farmer waited anxiously as the sage sat with the young woman for a long time. He came out, shaking his head.

"It is a very serious condition, I'm afraid," he said. "The worst case I have ever seen."

"Is there no remedy?" asked the farmer anxiously.

The sage sighed. "There is one thing that may cure her, but it is very difficult to obtain."

"Tell me, please," said the farmer, wringing his hands. "We will try anything."

"High up the slopes of the mountain" said the sage, pointing with his staff, "There is a certain spring. The waters of this spring are life-giving. I believe that they may cure your wife of her sickness."

"But that's easy!" said the farmer in relief. "Just tell me where this spring is and I will go at first light and bring back the water!"

The sage shook his head. "It is not so easy as that, I'm afraid. You see, this water loses its power if it comes into contact with anything other than a human hand." He paused, looking sadly at the farmer. "You must climb the mountain, cup the water from the spring in your hands and bring it back here."

"I will!" shouted the young man.

At dawn of the following day he followed the sage up the winding path, across the river, through a dense forest and finally began to climb the steep slope that led to the summit. As the day wore on, the farmer's hopes began to fade. How could he possibly navigate this hostile terrain with water cupped in his hands? But he was young and full of love, so he set his face and continued.

The spring was at the opening to an underground cavern.

The water flowed out in a trickle and then disappeared into a tiny stream that ran away downhill. The sage watched as the young man filled his cupped hands with the cool water, and then waved him goodbye with his staff as the farmer stumbled away, his hands clutched so tightly together that his fingers showed white.

He managed to get no further than the first line of trees before tripping and falling face down, spilling what was left of the water in his hands. Angrily, he rose and retraced his steps to the spring. The second attempt saw him safely through the trees, but he found he could not descend the slope without balancing. Finally, nearly falling from a rocky path, he threw out his hands to catch himself, spilling the precious fluid at his feet.

He went back again, and this time managed to traverse the slope and the forest, but when he arrived into open country, and could just about see his home in the distance, he noticed that despite his efforts, the sun was evaporating the little trickle of water left in his hands. He began to run, hoping that a few precious drops would remain when he reached the door.

Dark was falling when he came stumbling across the front garden of his home. He was scratched raw by wounds from branches. His body quivered with exhaustion. His cupped hands had lost all sensation. It was too dark even to see if any drops still lay in his hands. He pushed open the door with his shoulder and staggered to his wife's bedside. He held out his hands for her, and then saw despairingly that there was not even a single drop for her to drink. She placed his hands on either side of her face for a moment and fell asleep.

The next morning the farmer awoke to an unusual sound, one he had not heard for weeks. It was his wife humming a tune as she began preparing his breakfast. Incredulous, he sat up in bed as he watched her come into the room with a steaming cup of tea. He reached out, and his sore hands cupped hers. His eyes were full of questions, but his wife just smiled.

"The sage knew it all along," she said, gazing at him, perhaps for the first time, with love. "It wasn't the magic water at all. It was the vessel that carried it."

No Vacancy in Heaven

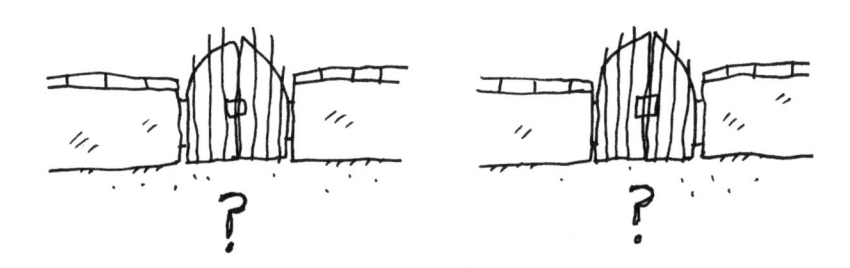

A man woke up dead. At first, he didn't remember that he had died, the crash had been so sudden. Then he found himself walking along a road with another man. Gradually he realised that his companion was the driver of the other car. They were walking through countryside on what seemed a pleasant spring day. After a few minutes, they began to chat.

"So, how are you finding it so far?" he asked his companion.

"Not too bad. Better than I expected, anyway. But what do you reckon we're supposed to do? I'm getting a little thirsty."

"Me too. I guess we need to find some water." He pointed at what appeared to be a large, white wall that grew out of the landscape. It was so large that he couldn't see the end of it. "Let's ask someone over there," he said.

After a very long walk alongside the wall, they found a gate. It was made of gold, or some shiny metal, and, sure enough, there was an ornate sign over the grillwork that said

"Heaven" in fancy letters. Another sign said, "Ring bell for entry". They pulled a velvet rope and heard a distant bell clang.

An old man in a white robe and a beard that fell almost to his waist appeared. "Yes?" he said.

"We were wondering if you had some water," said the man's companion. "But while we're at it—could we come into heaven?"

"Plenty of water inside," said the old man. "But, I'm sorry to announce that after ten million years of operation, heaven is almost full. In fact, we have only one vacancy. So one of you can enter, but the other one cannot."

"Let's go over here and talk this over," said the companion. The first man turned his back, and in a flash the companion dashed inside. The old man pulled the door shut and hung a sign that read, "No Vacancy." The companion shrugged as he was being led away, as if to say, "Nothing personal. Just business."

The man was disappointed. He continued his walk alone, becoming gradually more and more thirsty. After some hours he saw another large wall and a gate, though this one had no sign over the entrance. A cheerful attendant was polishing the railings. He smiled as the man approached.

The man explained that he was thirsty, and the attendant said, "Come inside. Plenty of water in Heaven."

"Heaven?" said the man. "But I passed Heaven several hours ago. They were full up."

"Oh, that wasn't heaven," said the attendant. "That's the other place. We're the real article here, and we have plenty of room."

"But, doesn't that annoy you—that they claim to be Heaven?"

"No," said the attendant, smiling cheerfully. "We encourage it, because it weeds out all those who would abandon their friends."

The Missing Half Hour

Tom, a young man of a large family, was always half an hour late. He had tried to overcome this affliction for many years, by tying strings to his fingers and buying watches that he wore up and down his arm. Some of these had alarms, so that when you were standing next to him he would suddenly start ringing or buzzing, but even this didn't help. He would forget what the errand was that had made him set the alarm in the first place, and when he remembered—even though he hurried—he still arrived half an hour late. Because of this he had never been able to hold down a job for long and he was the disgrace of his family.

The family were all ashamed of him, and each time he failed to appear on time, his six older brothers and sisters would all shout at him, call him useless and leave him crying alone in his room. They gave him his nickname, and soon everyone in the village knew it. He had become Tom the Tardy.

At last, Tom went to the home of a certain rabbi who was renowned for being able to solve people's personal problems. He begged the rabbi to help him overcome his tardiness, to give him some lesson or prayer that he could memorise and thereby start arriving on time. The rabbi heard Tom's story in silence.

"Why is it so important that you become punctual?" he asked finally.

"Why, so that my brothers and sisters will respect me," Tom said. "If I learned to be on time, then I could have a job just as they do and they would think more of me."

"I will help you," said the rabbi. Ask all of them to come here to meet us here at exactly six o'clock this afternoon."

Overjoyed, Tom went to each of his siblings and told them what the rabbi had said. All of them agreed, but with a sour face. They knew Tardy Tom was beyond any help.

Tom spent the afternoon in eager expectation. The hours passed slowly. Then, looking at one of his many watches, he realised that it was already five to six! Racing across town, he got caught in the tangle of tents at the market and blocked by a flock of sheep that a careless shepherd had allowed to stray into the road. He stumbled in his haste, and so arrived, scratched and dishevelled, at exactly six-thirty.

All the brothers and sisters were sitting with the Rabbi in his study. When Tom entered, they immediately began shouting at him. "You can't even be on time for such an important meeting as this! You're hopeless! We might as well go home!" And as usual, Tom sank into a chair, mumbling apologies and burying his face in his hands.

The rabbi spoke: "I have discovered the root of Tom's

problem. You see, he is not actually late at all, but on time."

"What can you mean, Rabbi?" asked the eldest brother. "He is clearly 30 minutes late!"

The rabbi continued. "By an accident of fate, Tom has been robbed of half an hour. This happened before or soon after his birth—only God knows that. It is this missing half hour that accounts for what you all see as tardiness."

The brothers and sisters were silent in amazement. This was a wise man telling them something so strange that they found it difficult to accept. At last one of the sisters, nearest in age to Tom, asked, "What can be done about it?"

The rabbi beamed. "You all know that family must take care of one another, share their wealth with each member. It so happens that each of you have a normal amount of time. So I ask you to share some of it with your brother. Not much—just five minutes each."

He told each of them to come forward and to place their hands upon Tom's head, one by one. They were instructed to concentrate on giving the lad a free gift of five minutes. In the silence of the study, punctuated only by the ticking of the rabbi's clock, they did this. As each one placed a hand on Tom's head, their expressions changed. When they had finished, there was no longer any harshness to be felt in the room, and Tom's face wore a smile. From that day, he was never late again.

The rabbi was smiling too. He knew how valuable five minutes of someone's time can be.

The Churn

A spiritual teacher was approached by a well-dressed man one day as he was helping with the farm chores on his ashram. Without an introduction, the man said, in a challenging voice, "If you are such a great teacher, answer me two questions."

The teacher smiled. "I can answer them better if you reveal what the questions are."

"The first one is this: if God exists, why can't I see Him? The second is, why must life be so hard?"

The master pointed to a churn which had been filled with milk. "Look in there. What do you see?"

"Milk, of course," replied the seeker.

"Now grab the handle and start pumping," said the master.

The seeker began working the churn. He made several comments and complaints, but the master didn't reply. He began to perspire, and after a while he stopped.

"What is the point of this?" he asked crossly. "I'm a banker, not a farmer."

"Look inside again. What do you see?" the master said.

"I see butter," said the man.

"And why couldn't you see the butter before?"

"Because it was still in the milk."

"That answers your first question," said the master.

"All right. I see your point. But what about my second question? Why is life so hard?"

The master didn't reply. He just handed the man the handle of the churn. And smiled.

On Your Bike

There was a great Zen teacher who invited five of his best students to his home. All arrived riding their bicycles. When they had dismounted, the teacher asked them, "Why are you riding your bicycles?"

The first student replied, "I need my bicycle to more easily carry all these books I read about enlightenment."

The teacher said, "Continue studying until you become wise. Sit here, at my feet."

The second student replied, "I ride my bicycle because I love to look at the beautiful scenery as I pass through." The teacher praised the student: "You are developing aesthetic sensibility. Sit here at my feet."

The third student replied, "When I ride my bicycle, I am able to forget other things and chant the sacred mantra." The teacher congratulated the student, "Your practice will one day liberate you. Sit here at my feet."

The fourth student answered, "Riding my bicycle, I feel in touch with all nature and all beings." The teacher smiled and said, "You are learning the path of compassion. Sit here at my feet."

When questioned, the last student said, "I ride my bicycle to ride my bicycle." Without a word, the teacher went over and sat at his feet.

The Well Trained Ass

Travelling along a high mountain road, a pilgrim happened upon a man riding a small donkey. He was beating the animal with a look of frustration on his face, but the ass appeared hardly to notice.

"Good morning," said the pilgrim. "Why are you beating your donkey, may I ask?"

"You may ask," said the man, sweating from his exertions. "I'm beating him because he's so slow. He's very stubborn, you see, which is why I'm getting rid of him this very afternoon."

"Ah, so you're taking him to market in the city? Excellent! May I travel with you?"

The two men started out, the pilgrim walking but able to keep up with the donkey's pace. The man continued slapping at the beast with a leather strap.

"Why are you in such a hurry?" asked the pilgrim.

"Because I want to get to the market before it closes. I don't want to be stuck in these mountains after nightfall."

A mile or so down the road they spotted a man emerging from the dense forest. He was carrying an axe and a large bundle of freshly cut branches across his back. He stopped and greeted the two.

"Where are you off to in such a hurry?" he asked the rider.

"I need to be at the city market before nightfall," said the man, wiping his brow.

"Oh, I wouldn't recommend that," said the woodcutter. "Haven't you heard? The king has decreed that no strangers may be admitted before sundown. You might wind up in a cell if you get there too early."

"Thanks for your advice," said the rider. "We must slow our pace and wait until the market opens tomorrow."

They set out again. After a few paces the man started beating his donkey once again.

"Why are you beating him now?" asked the pilgrim. "We no longer have any hurry."

"Because he's travelling too quickly," said the frustrated rider. "Can't you see how he's defying me?"

The pilgrim said nothing, but observed that the donkey's gait was unchanged from a few minutes before. Just after midday they saw a man, his wife and their three children coming toward them in the opposite direction. They were singing and seemed happy. When they stopped to exchange greetings, the pilgrim asked what was responsible for their high spirits.

"Haven't you heard? The old king has been deposed, and since yesterday the gates of the city are open to us all. We are free to visit our relatives for the first time in years."

"After they had departed, the rider grumbled, "Well, we still won't make it by evening now."

They started again as the sun cleared the mountain peaks and cast its golden light on the lush forests. Birds wheeled and soared, and wildflowers spread a thick carpet on the open land. The pilgrim and the rider spoke of many things. They stopped and shared their bread and cheese, and each had half of an apple. The donkey grazed contentedly at the verges. The beauty of the afternoon filled them all, and when they set off again the rider was calm and did not beat his donkey, though his plodding pace was unchanged.

Just as the sun touched the western horizon they arrived at the city gates, which were standing open and unguarded. The rider stopped and wheeled his donkey about.

"Here we must part, Pilgrim," he said, offering his hand.

"Why, aren't you going to market?" asked the pilgrim, astonished.

"To sell this donkey?" said the rider earnestly. "Why should I, now that I've got him so well-trained?"

The Dimmest Lantern

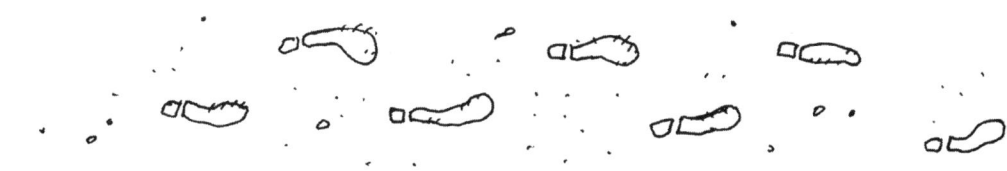

A traveller was walking hurriedly along the edge of a dark wood when he broke the strap of his shoe. He sat for a long time beside the road and finally managed to repair it. By that time, however, it was growing dark. Reaching the village he was travelling to would take too long. He would certainly have to make the journey in the dark. But the road was unknown to him and treacherous, with many stones over which he could stumble and potholes into which he could fall.

Hurrying as best he could, he started out along the road. The sun dipped below the horizon and he nearly stumbled several times. Finally, in despair, he sat on a rock. With no torch to guide him, he knew he couldn't reach his destination. As the shadows closed in he began to hear noises. He had heard tales that there were fierce wolves that prowled these parts. Maybe he was being stalked even now. Though the night was not cold, a chill ran through him.

One of the noises seemed to be getting louder. The traveller peered into the darkness and saw what seemed to be a pair of glowing eyes. He hid behind a rock, knowing that that wouldn't be of any use if a wolf was after him. As the noises grew louder he saw that what he had thought were eyes was actually a very dim lantern. The noises became human footsteps. A person was approaching along the path.

Fearful that it might be a brigand, the traveller stayed in his hiding place. As the stranger approached, he realised that his foot was visible from the road. He pulled it back hurriedly and knocked loose a small stone that was balanced on the edge of his rock. The footsteps stopped. The stranger raised the lantern, which was only a small candle behind glass.

"Hey!" said a voice. "What are you doing crouched back there?"

Knowing he had been discovered, the traveller stood up. The stranger was an old man, much shorter and frailer than he.

"I was hiding in case you were a brigand," he said ashamedly.

"A brigand!" the man cackled. "I'm no brigand. I'm a philosopher."

"Where are you headed?" asked the traveller. He was glad to be able to see anything at all, even if the lantern was very dim.

"There is only one place to go on this road," said the philosopher wryly. "To the next place."

"Well, could I walk with you then?" asked the traveller. "Your lantern is very dim, but it's better than the darkness."

They set out together. The lantern cast a small pool of light, so that they couldn't see more than a single step ahead of them. This made them walk very slowly, and as they walked, they talked.

"What sort of philosophy do you do?" asked the traveller.

"Any sort that's necessary," said the philosopher. "I never know what's ahead, so I just philosophise as the mood strikes me."

"And that's how you live?" asked the traveller. "Just… philosophising?"

"There is always a market for good philosophy," was the reply.

Once or twice the two men stopped. The traveller shared some bread he had in his satchel, and the philosopher carefully divided an apple from his. The light of the lantern was like a small bubble that contained them both. Nothing could be seen beyond its glow on the cloudy, moonless night. Inside it seemed very safe. The traveller forgot about what lay beyond the light..

At last the first rays of dawn appeared on the horizon. The bubble around them expanded, and for the first time the traveller could see where they had been walking. They were on the edge of a very steep cliff, one over which the traveller would surely have fallen without the dim lantern's glow.

"Look!" he shouted. "Did you know we were walking along a cliff?"

"Of course," replied the philosopher. "There are many cliffs around here."

"But it could have been dangerous! We could have fallen!"

"We could see well where to plant our feet, by walking slowly," said the philosopher.

"But we could only see one step at a time," the traveller protested.

"Tell me, how many steps can you take at one time?" the philosopher asked. He was smiling and looked as if he might burst out laughing at any moment. The traveller was speechless, staring at his companion.

"I told you I was a philosopher," he said.

The Gift of the Sky

The sky maiden was called Celine. Everything about her was air-kissed, and legend compared her long yellow hair to sunbeams and the pale blue of her eyes to the colour of the skies just after the sun has made its morning ascent. As a sky maiden, things of the earth did not seem to affect her. She stepped lightly over the ground like someone who is only touching down out of politeness, and not because gravity held sway over her. Everything about her seemed to whisper that she was only visiting.

The place where the earth touches the sky is called the horizon, and that is where she was first seen among the farthest hills that stretch the vision of the earthbound, and that is where her suitor, a young man who tended sheep, first lost his heart and his reason. Shepherds prefer the rough crags of the horizon. They are never comfortable in the ruts and roads of towns. That is why rude whispers accompany them and why sometimes they are even feared.

He saw her first as she walked lightly down from a stony

peak that could not be climbed by men, though many had tried and died in the attempt. When she glanced at him, seeming to see not his form, but the frozen light that composed it, she approached.

"You are a man of the earth," she said, as though it was a question.

"And you?" he asked, hardly daring to hear the answer.

"I am a child of the sky. I have been sent to renew the harmony between your world and mine, so that the Great Purpose is not lost."

"How will you do that?" asked the shepherd, trembling.

"I will wed a man of this world, and our union will ensure the harmony of both."

Stricken with love, the shepherd said, "May I dare hope that it is I who will marry you?"

Celine said nothing, as if she were listening to someone speaking invisibly in her ear. She looked at the shepherd's face and nodded.

"That depends upon our courtship. We must exchange gifts for our engagement, and if they are deemed suitable by both, my father will give his blessing."

"And how will we know if they are suitable?"

Celine smiled, and it as if the sun had shone from behind a cloud. "Look at me well, man of the earth. Select a gift for me, one that will win my heart. In one week we will meet here again and exchange these tokens of our troth."

Then she was gone, seeming to glide up the rough cliffs

until she had vanished in the clouds.

The shepherd went to town, wondering if he had gone mad, but afraid to awake from this lovely dream. He immediately sold his flock, then went to his family and friends to beg more money to purchase a gift for the sky maiden, whose image now haunted his waking thoughts and tormented his dreams. When he had amassed the largest possible sum of money, he went to a goldsmith in the city and commissioned a work of the finest gold for his gift. He pressed and harried the craftsman for five days, and on the last day he emerged with an engraved box of the finest sandalwood, containing his token of love.

They met again where the sky nearly touches the earth. Celine appeared to him even more radiant, if it were possible. Her face wore an enigmatic smile, her eyes glowed with the promise of love. Trembling, he went to one knee and held out the sandalwood box. She took it and loosed the clasp, pulling from within a small golden globe, an image of the world. It lay in her hand with unaccustomed weight.

"It is certainly a thing of this world," she said. "And it is beautiful to me, although strange."

Then she presented him with a small chest, fashioned of some material unknown to him. It seemed to be the stuff that forms the feathers of birds. He opened it slowly, feeling the lightness of the thing, as if it were only partly real. He looked inside, and an expression of puzzlement drew his features.

"It is a box of great loveliness," he said. "But there is nothing inside!"

The shy maiden's face ceased to glow. She put the golden ball back into its box and held it out for the shepherd. Something in the air darkened, as if the clouds of a storm had appeared in a cloudless sky.

"Goodbye," she said, with a trace of sadness, as she turned to go back up the unscalable hill.

"But..." said the shepherd, "I do not understand. Was my gift unacceptable? It was the most precious thing I could buy."

She turned and looked at him as if from a great distance.

"And mine was the most precious thing I possess as well. Something you could neither see nor appreciate."

So even today the heavens and earth remain divided. And too late the shepherd realised that what she had given him was a box full of sky.

The Last Words

Word went out from the palace that the health of the great sage was beginning to fail. This alarmed the whole of the kingdom which had relied for many years on the old man's wisdom and experience. People became distracted. They began to stop what they were doing in mid-reach. Lawns went un-mowed, pies were left too long in the oven. Children forgot to play. Nobody could imagine what would happen to them without the sage's presence.

As the old man neared his end, his courtiers and adherents began to plan for his succession. Someone new would have to be found, and somehow the secret of the old man's wisdom would have to be transmitted to a new generation. They looked at each other without much enthusiasm. None of them seemed up to the task.

As death approached, the sage requested that a great public meeting be held, at which he would make his last thoughts known to the world. Invitations were hurriedly written, and on the appointed day the great hall of the palace was filled with the great and the good of the kingdom. Places near the front, where the sage would be carried onto a dais, were reserved for the wealthy landowners and politicians. Behind them were the merchants and professionals, and then the most respectable of home owners, all scrubbed and washed and wearing their best clothes. Ordinary people, farmers and carpenters and blacksmiths, had to sit in rows on the lawn. While they awaited the appearance of the sage, tea was served by a few young women from the town, who weaved among the rows of dignitaries carrying large silver trays.

At last the chief courtier stood on the dais until the hubbub of excited talk died down. He raised a hand to still the last whispers and announced that the sage would be too ill to walk, and would be carried on a litter. When the sorrowful procession of litter-bearers entered the hall, everyone stood reverently. The sage lay, his head propped up on a brocade cushion. Those nearest to him could see that, oddly, he was wearing a smile.

The chief courtier bent over the old man and quickly announced that it was now time for the sage's last words. There was no sound to be heard. Even the flies had stopped droning in the still air. The courtier's booming voice rang out, "Tell, us O great one—what is the secret of your wisdom?"

Slowly the sage raised a single finger, as if pointing upward towards the heavens. Everyone bent forward, straining to catch his feeble words.

"Listen carefully…" croaked the sage. There was a pause. The finger dropped, the old eyes closed for the last time, but the smile remained on his face. The courtiers and doctors bent over him, and at last the chief courtier stood and addressed the crowd.

"I'm sorry to report that our revered sage has passed away," he said. There was a collective gasp from the room. "And, sadly, he did so without giving us his last words…"

A roar of disquiet and disbelief filled the room. There was so much noise that no one could hear the small voice of a serving girl. She said, "But he did give us his wise last words! He did!"

Unfortunately, no one was listening.

You're Welcome

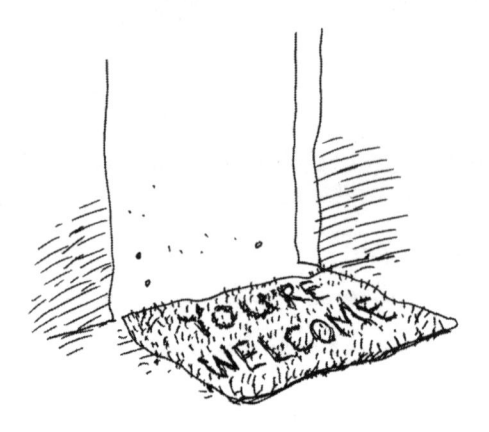

An ambitious merchant bought a piece of property for development. The vendor signed the deed, then said, "Oh, I forgot to mention. The old man next door has built his house at the edge of his property and a few inches of the corner is actually on my land. I never minded, so I'm sure you won't."

The merchant went straight to the property to look again. The house next door was small and tidy, and there was a small queue of people waiting at the door. Curious, he asked what they were waiting for.

"We're waiting to see the holy man," one of them said. "We've come for his blessing."

The merchant watched for a while. He couldn't understand what all the fuss was about. Then it occurred to him that the so-called holy man must be cleverly extracting money from his visitors. Never one to miss out on a potential profit, he waited until there was no one at the door and knocked. After a moment a small man opened the door. He was smiling, and stood aside to admit the visitor.

"I'm not here for your blessing," snapped the merchant. "I am the owner of the land next door. Part of your house sits on my property, and I am here to collect rent or it will have to be destroyed."

"Rent?" said the old man. "But I don't have much money."

The merchant scowled. "I will return in one hour. If you do not produce two pieces of gold, I will order the court to evict you from my land."

An hour later he was back. The old man carried a knotted handkerchief with small copper coins inside. "I believe these are the equivalent of two gold pieces," he said, and extended the bundle. The merchant took it from his hand, and as he did, the old man said, "Thank you."

The merchant puzzled at this remark. Why would the old charlatan thank him? The next day he was back. "I have come for more rent money," he said. The old man looked at him for a moment. "I have no more money, but perhaps something I possess will do instead." He stood aside, and the merchant went in. The place was simple and bare, and there was very little in the way of ornamentation. He spied a picture in a gilt frame on the mantle. It might bring a little money in the marketplace. "I'll have that frame," he said.

The old man removed the picture of what must have been his late wife and gave the merchant the frame. "Thank you," he said.

That night the merchant couldn't sleep. Why was the man

thanking him? He returned early the next morning and told the man that he had one more rent payment to make. Without a word, the old man removed his shoes and coat and handed them over. "Thank you," he said again.

The merchant went away, his head reeling. Was this some elaborate ruse to make him lose his mind? He asked a few people who stood in the queue why he would say such a thing. "Why, he's a spiritual man," said one woman. "No doubt he feels that possessions and wealth are a burden that you are removing from his shoulders."

After another sleepless night the merchant returned. When the old man opened his door, he thrust the little sack of money, the picture frame and the clothing into his arms. "Take this back!" he nearly shouted.

The old man looked at the possessions in his arms and then at the face of the merchant.

"You're welcome," he said.

The Teacher of Jade

WAYS TO LOOK AT JADE

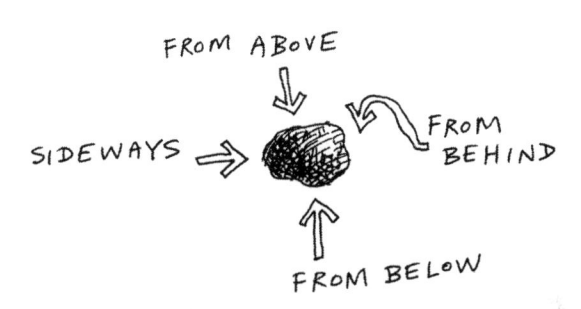

FROM ABOVE
SIDEWAYS →
FROM BEHIND
FROM BELOW

A merchant of Basra had succeeded so well in his business that he decided to devote himself to the finer arts of living. He cultivated his ear for music, for flower gardening and for enjoying the delicacies of the table. He became known for his wide variety of tastes and his grasp of aesthetics.

One day he was discussing his interests with a luncheon guest. The man happened to mention the inlaid stonework of a certain mosque in the city. He named a number of semi-precious stones that had been cut and inserted into the patterns at the bases of the minarets. The merchant found that he could not visualise the descriptions of the stones. Sensing a lack in himself, he resolved to do something about it. At the suggestion of his friend, he decided to start with the stone known as jade.

The merchant began a search for someone who could teach him about the subject. He made enquiries among his many acquaintances and customers, in the marketplace and among his neighbours. One day the barber was trimming his beard and told the merchant that he had heard of a certain man who claimed to be an authority on jade. Excitedly, the merchant dispatched a servant to the man's rooms and arranged a tutorial to begin on the first day of the following week.

On Monday at nine o'clock he presented himself, as arranged, at the man's house in the city. The teacher admitted him with courtesy but with very few words. He was shown into a bare room on the first floor and seated in a wooden chair. The teacher left and then returned carrying a lump of green stone, which he placed in the hands of the merchant. Then, without a word, he left the room.

The merchant sat alone, holding the stone. There was no sound, not even the noise of horses and carts passing in the street below. He turned the green mineral over and over in his hands until he grew bored. After two hours, realising that the teacher was not going to return, he rose, placed the stone on the chair and left the room. At the foot of the stairs he was surprised to find the teacher standing by the front door. As the merchant passed, he said, "Tomorrow, then. At the same time."

On the following morning the merchant considered not returning to the teacher's house. Nevertheless he appeared again at the appointed time.

Once again he was admitted courteously, but in silence. This time the teacher handed him a stone. This one was yellowish in cast, but in all other respects the same. After two hours the merchant left the stone on the chair, passed the teacher at the door and went home.

The following week the merchant was once again in the shop of the barber.

"Have you succeeded in your desire to understand jade?" the barber asked.

"Yes, I have," said the merchant, "Though I must say it was due to no excellence on the part of the teacher."

The barber pressed him further. "He was unsatisfactory, then?"

"Completely so," said the merchant. "Each day he simply handed me a stone and left me unattended. This went on for four days, with a green piece of jade, a lump of yellow jade, a small piece of grey jade and a mottled jade which has all the colours of the rainbow."

"And on Friday?" asked the barber.

"On Friday he handed me a lump of stone that any fool could see wasn't jade at all."

Based on a story told by Rev Derek Smith

Shrinking Monsters

The monster had gathered where it always had—on the hill overlooking the village. Its huge shadow could be seen by everyone at all times of day. Fear had gripped the people, and they turned to their spiritual leader for help.

But he had become an old man and was now too frail to rise from his bed. People took turns tending to his needs, and he looked at each of them closely, with a little smile on his face. The youngest, a girl, lingered longest at his bedside, arranging the flowers that so many had sent.

He beckoned to her to come near. He asked her why the people seemed so worried. She told him of the monster on the hill. He thought for a moment, then whispered in her ear.

The following morning the little girl arose early and started walking toward the path that led up the hill. People were startled; they asked he if she wasn't afraid.

"No," she said calmly. "Because the Wise One has told me

the monster's name. He said that once you know the name of something, you lose fear of it."

They watched as she began to climb the steep track. The shadow of the monster loomed hugely over her. Still she climbed, and as she got nearer, something odd happened: the shadow of the beast grew smaller. It shrank and shrank as she rose and rose, and then finally disappeared from sight. After a while the little girl came down from the hill.

"Where is the monster?" everyone asked.

She patted the pocket of her apron. "He's in here," she said. "The poor thing is too frightened to come out." Everyone could see a small—a very small pair of eyes peering out fearfully from her apron.

"But how did you make him shrink?" they asked.

"It was simple," said the girl. "The Wise One told me that this monster is the only one in the world that shrinks as you get to him. He told me his name. I called it out as I got closer."

"And what is his name?" they all asked.

"But it was the tiny squeak of the monster's voice that gave them the answer. "My name," the monster said, "Is 'What Might Happen.'"

I Have Not Yet Sold My Shop

A poor shopkeeper of Mumbai had always wanted to find spiritual enlightenment. He had read scores of religious books, done puja at innumerable temples, and sat for long periods in meditation. Finally, after years of searching, he met a guru who, he was certain, would lead him on the spiritual path.

He sat in devotion as the master led prayers and gave discourses that thrilled the hundreds of people who came to see him. He was a gentle man of no worldly wealth with a look of loving attention to all he met. The shopkeeper decided to devote his life to following in this man's footsteps.

One day he heard that the guru was leaving the city to open an ashram in a rural town a day's travel away. The shopkeeper was worried; how could he maintain his relationship with the master if he was so far away? Troubled, he sought an audience with the guru.

"Master," he said, "You know that I am devoted to your teachings, and that I long to be near you."

"Yes," replied the master, looking at him with kindness.

"But I am a shopkeeper, dependent upon my business for my livelihood, and you are going to be far away."

The master was silent for a moment, then said, "Why don't you sell your shop and come to live with us?"

"I would dearly love to, Master," said the shopkeeper. "But it is just a poor stall that sells trinkets, hardly wide enough for two to sit side by side. Who would buy it from me?"

"I will help you," said the master. "But you must obey my instructions implicitly."

Overjoyed, the shopkeeper said, "Then what must I do? Anything you ask would be too little."

"Just one thing," said the master. "Every time you encounter another person, in whatever situation, before you say another word, you must say, 'I have not yet sold my shop'."

"But, Master, even before saying 'hello'?"

"Before all," repeated the guru, smiling.

The shopkeeper began at once. Whenever he was greeted in the street, before even saying "hello", he said, "I have not yet sold my shop." When a customer came to his counter, when he naturally would have begun sales pitch about the exceptional quality and low price of his goods, he would first say "I have not yet sold my shop." People began to laugh behind his back. He heard this, but, remembering the words of his guru, persisted. But still no offers were forthcoming; after weeks his shop remained unsold.

The shopkeeper was a man of little means, but he had a cousin who had made a fortune in the export trade. The cousin lived in a stately mansion on the outskirts of the city, surrounded by high walls and staffed by many servants. He had always maintained good relations with the family, as anyone might with rich relations.

One day he heard that his cousin had died suddenly, and that the funeral was to be held the very next day. His invitation arrived by a bemused courier, who was greeted, as always, with the words, "I have not yet sold my shop."

The shopkeeper could not sleep that night. He would have to give his commiserations to the family of his cousin; it would be unthinkable not to. But he was under orders. He thought to ask the guru for a special dispensation, but the master and his party had already moved away. In the morning, full of dread, he dressed in his best clothes and set off for the temple where the funeral was being held.

It was just as he feared. At the end of the ceremony, mourners passed by the line of family members, including the grieving widow. He joined the queue, and as he approached the widow, his heart sank. At last it was his turn. He took the woman's hand, and, remembering the words of his guru, burst out, "I have not yet sold my shop!"

There was silence for a moment, as if everyone had heard his rude and extraordinary words. He was at the point of gushing out his proper sentiments when the widow smiled and said, "What an extraordinary co-incidence! It so happens that my husband's valet is at the point of retirement and is looking for just such a small enterprise. I would be delighted to purchase your shop for him as a parting gift. We can arrange the sale straight away."

The handkerchief went back to her eyes. "Thank you for coming," she said.

The Cries of the Poor

A rich man was travelling through a forest when he was set upon by thieves. A hermit who lived alone heard the noise and ran toward the place where the attack was taking place. The thieves, fearing that it might be soldiers, ran away. The hermit cleaned the wounds of the rich man and gave him a place to stay in his hut.

The next morning the rich man expressed his gratitude. "Tell me what you want," he said, "Anything. I will give it to you."

"But it was nothing. I did it for my sake. I have never been able to bear the cries of the afflicted."

The rich man insisted. "Such selflessness demands a reward. Tell me what you need."

The hermit thought, and then said, "I can't think of anything, I'm afraid. I have all I need."

"Then if the need ever arises, you must come and tell me.

You are entitled to a reward."

Years passed. The hermit was getting older, and his cow stopped producing milk. A new cow cost ten silver coins. He counted what he had and found eight. He remembered the rich man's offer and decided to ask him for the two that he lacked.

He travelled to the city and found the rich man's mansion. After some explanation, he was allowed in and told to wait in an anteroom beside the rich man's office. Through the door he could hear the conversation of the rich man and several of his lawyers.

"If you want to buy the last estate in the valley, you will need an additional million gold coins," said one lawyer. "But you have only half a million in liquid funds at the moment," said another. The rich man groaned. "What am I going to do?" he asked.

The hermit found the servant who had admitted him. He handed his bundle of eight silver coins to the man and said, "Please give these to your master. It isn't much, but perhaps it may help. I have never been able to ignore the cries of the poor."

How to Make Pots

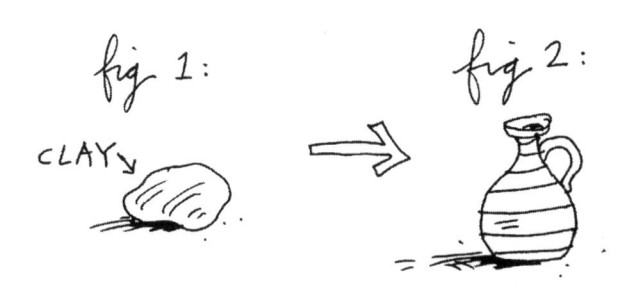

fig. 1: CLAY ⇒ *fig. 2:* [jug]

The spiritual teacher was very famous, and many seekers after truth waited years to spend time with him. One of these was a potter from a distant city who was delighted, after several years, to receive an invitation. He arrived at dusk, and after a pleasant but simple meal with the master, slept soundly.

The following morning after tea, the master summoned him. He found him standing beside the road with his staff in his hand. "Let's walk," the master said. They set out and wandered through the fields and villages for hours. The master would stop and greet people and hear what they had to say. He would play with village children and toss a ball for village dogs. Sometimes he stood quietly watching the light change over the hills. At sundown they returned to the ashram, had a simple meal and retired.

The next day was a repeat of the first. The master walked and talked to people, played with children and dogs and watched the sun move overhead. The potter became frustrated because there were no philosophical discourses, no meditation instruction and no lessons. After two more days, with his allotted week slipping away, he confronted the master.

"Great One, "he said, "I am concerned that my long-awaited week is fast going, and still I have not had any spiritual instruction from Your Eminence."

The master did not reply, but set out on another of his daily walks with the potter lagging behind. As the day passed, the potter became even more frustrated. "Could you not at least write down some of the spiritual realities for me? Something I can read later and learn about the spiritual path?"

"An excellent idea!" said the master. "Let's make a trade. I have always wanted to make pottery. Why don't you give me a complete written account of how to make fine pots, and I will give you a complete set of instructions on how to realise the Self."

"But that is impossible, Eminence!" the potter cried. "It has taken me many years of practice. I know in my fingers how the clay should feel, how to kick the wheel at just the right speed, how to decorate the pots and make sure they survive the firing afterwards. I could never explain all that in a book!

The master smiled. "You have just answered your own question," he said.

Alchemy

An old man, a successful farmer, had a beautiful daughter, whom he married off to the cleverest young man in town. At first the couple were happy, because they were living well off the girl's dowry. Then the funds started to run out, but instead of working as any other new husband would have done, he locked himself in his shed and began to try to turn base metals into gold. He thought he was clever enough to become the first real alchemist.

When the father learned this, he called his daughter to him. He couldn't help noticing that she looked a bit thin and pale, and that her clothes were showing signs of wear. He got the whole story from her, but instead of frowning, he smiled and told her, "Send him to me."

When the husband turned up, worried and reluctant, he was met by a friendly father-in-law. "I'm delighted to hear that you're an alchemist," he said. "I was one myself when I was young. In fact, I learned the secret of turning lead into gold."

"You did?" said the young man. "But you must share your

knowledge with me."

"Unfortunately, I couldn't proceed with the process because I began to grow older and the process takes a lot of work and energy."

"I am young and able," said the son-in-law. "I could manage any amount of hard work."

The father said that he was willing to teach the young man to become a true alchemist. He told him his great secret. The missing ingredient was the fine silver dust that collects on the leaves of banana trees. But the dust is very fine, and the amount required was a kilo.

"That will mean hundreds and hundreds of plants," said the son-in-law. "And I have none."

"I will lend you the money as an investment," said the father. "You can repay me from the wealth you will surely gain."

So the young man bought land, cleared and fertilised it and planted hundreds of banana trees. He tended the plants very carefully, so that they would grow large quantities of the silver dust. Slowly he collected the powder. After seven years, he had collected a kilo of the powder. He took his wife and went to see the old alchemist, carrying the powder in a sealed jar.

"Marvellous!" said the old man. He took the jar and carefully opened it. Then he seemed to stumble, and the powder fell onto the ground, where a gust of wind carried it all away.

"Oh no!" cried the husband. "The work of seven years is lost!"

"Is it?" asked the old man. "Tell me—what do you do with the banana crops that your trees have produced over the years?"

"Why, we sell them, of course."

"And have you profited from that?" asked the old man.

"Yes, there has been no hunger in our house for seven years."

The old man smiled and said, "Sometimes it is the cleverest among us who cannot see what is before his eyes. You are prosperous, you have repaid your debt and you have wealth to leave your children."

"And so that is..?"

"You have turned worthless dust into gold. That is alchemy," said the father.

Give Everything

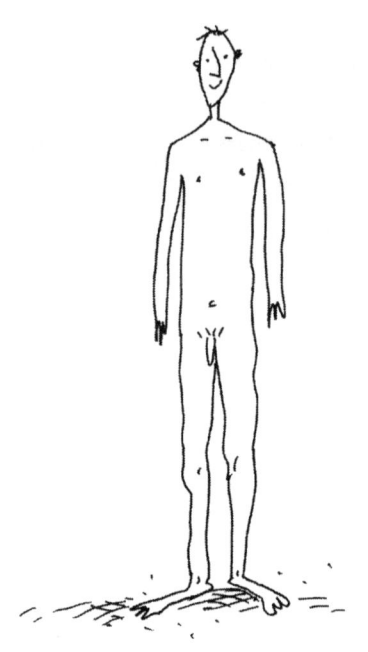

A householder, upon reaching his fiftieth birthday, resolved to leave behind the cares of family life and become a seeker after truth. Not far away was the seat of a master, whose spiritual wisdom was legendary. He made arrangements for the care of his wife and children and then travelled the short distance to the master's home.

He found the master sitting beneath a tree, stroking a contented-looking cat at his side. The householder approached humbly, removing his hat.

"Great One, I have decided to abandon earthly cares and seek enlightenment. I have come to ask for your help."

"That is a good thing indeed," said the master. "And what

are you prepared to give up in order to attain your goal?"

"I will give up anything," said the man fervently.

"Anything?"

Yes, Wise One. You need but ask."

"Would you give up delicious food?"

"Yes."

"Drink? Sexual desire?"

"In a heartbeat, Master."

"Would you sacrifice your life?"

"Oh yes."

The master looked into his eyes for a moment, then smiled and said, "Nothing so drastic is necessary. I will ask you to do a very small thing, much less expensive than losing one's life."

"Anything," said the householder earnestly.

"Then please remove all your clothes and walk through the streets of the town for an hour."

"But, Great One, I cannot do that!" said the man in shock.

"Why not?" asked the master gently.

"Because it is shameful! Because people would look upon me as a madman!"

Hafiz is reported to have said: You cannot set foot upon the spiritual path until you have been chased out of town as a madman.

The Wrong Fox

WHICH IS THE WRONG FOX?

    A spiritual teacher was walking through the forest with a young disciple when they came upon an unusual sight. A fox had his hind leg wedged into a crevice in a large rock and was clearly trapped. He wasn't struggling, but was utterly calm, as if he had been there for some time. The teacher pulled the young man into the undergrowth, and putting his finger to his lips gestured that they should watch.

    After half an hour another fox appeared, carrying a field mouse in its mouth. The second fox sat beside the trapped one and dropped the mouse so that the other could eat. When the trapped fox had finished, the second sniffed him for a moment and then trotted away. The master found a large stick and approached the trapped fox, who snarled and writhed in fear. The disciple thought at first that the master was going to dispatch the fox and thereby relieve him of his misery, but instead, he shoved the stick into the crevice, and with great effort, pried it open enough for the fox to escape.

    The animal ran off limping slightly. The master walked on

with the disciple.

"Have you learned from the fox we saw?"

"Yes, Master," said the disciple. "I have learned a great spiritual lesson."

"Are you sure?" asked the Master.

"Yes. Very sure," said the disciple.

"Then go and live it," said the master.

Time passed, and the disciple returned to his home village. The master had no news of him for more than a year. One day he was travelling through a nearby region and decided to look up the young man. When he enquired, he was told that the disciple had become an idle person who lived by begging.

The master sought him out. The young man was unkempt and a little overweight, stretched out on a mat under a shade tree. As people passed, he held out his hand for donations.

Sighing, the master approached him, and without greeting said, "I thought you had learned a spiritual lesson from the foxes."

"Oh, but I have!" said the young man. "The trapped fox did nothing, and yet he was taken care of. I learned that if you trust in God, He will take care of all your needs. That is why I have become a beggar."

The master shook his head sadly. "You chose the wrong fox."

The Peach Seed Necklace

The old man always wore a leather thong around his neck, from which hung a peach pit. It was so old and so often touched that the ridges had nearly worn smooth. He was known in his village as an exceptionally kind man, a widower of many years who took special pains to help the young people as they were making their difficult passages into adulthood.

One clever young man, who had been wrestling with questions about his future, went to visit the old man. He was tall and handsome, and things that were difficult for others came easily to him. They sat together, watching the sun dip toward the horizon. The old man told stories and listened with concentration to what the young man had to say. By late afternoon the young man's questions had lost their sense of urgency, and had become absorbed into the peace that seemed to surround the old man.

"Why do you wear that peach pit?" the young man asked at last.

"Because it reminds me of who I am," smiled his senior, fondling the necklace. His eyes crinkled. "Have you time for one more story?" he asked.

The old man had not always been a bent, white-bearded figure, he said. As a youngster, he had been strong and clever. So clever and so attractive that he had learned early that he could always have what he wanted. If he couldn't charm things out of people, or trick them into obliging his desires, he would simply steal.

As time went by he grew worse and worse, finally being reduced to the status of a common thief, albeit a successful one. And then something happened: he fell in love.

The object of his devotion was a pretty young woman of a neighbouring village, whose family knew nothing of his tarnished reputation. He thought about her day and night. His heart swelled in his breast, and, as it did, he resolved to end his days of pilfering and deception and turn his hand to honest work. But before he could turn over this new leaf, he decided to commit one last crime.

A goldsmith in a nearby town had made an exquisite ring, embossed with the twined branches of a wild rose and hawthorn tree. This was displayed behind glass inside the doorway of his shop, and carefully watched over by the jeweller as he awaited a wealthy buyer. The lovelorn suitor mustered all his tricks, and, distracting the jeweller with his charm and quick wit, substituted a worthless band of brass for the ring and fled.

He was caught because the ring his bride wore at her wedding was unique, and tongues inevitably flapped. He was imprisoned and brought to trial before the lord of that kingdom in chains. He could offer no defence and no mitigating circumstances that would result in a pardon. Feeling his life had ended, he submitted to his humiliation and began his sentence in despair.

But the love that had nearly changed him would not let him rest. His days were spent pacing his cell and his nights twisting on his hard cot. He was allowed no visitors, and had no news of his bride. He hardly touched his meagre rations, but one day, as he looked at the remains of his porridge and the wilted peach that was his only meal, his mood changed. He knew that if he used his wiles to escape from imprisonment, that, for the first time in his life, he would be using them for good. He would save his bride from a life of loneliness and disgrace. He ate the peach and folded the pit into his palm.

The following morning he asked to see the lord, on the grounds of making restitution for his crime. His petition took several months, but in the end he was granted an audience with a tribunal composed of the lord and two deputies. He entered the chamber with his head hung low in subjugation. In his hand he clutched the peach pit.

The lord looked at him briefly, and said impatiently, "You have just five minutes, Thief, in which to make your case."

"Your Excellency," began the prisoner, "I have had many months to weigh my guilt in the cell, and I have decided to reveal certain facts that I was loath to relate at my trial."

"Go on," said the lord, shuffling papers on his desk.

"I knew that I was in possession of a treasure at the time

of my imprisonment, and so I felt that I would later be able to buy my freedom. But I have since learned that this treasure is unavailable to me because of my past crimes, and so I have decided to donate it to Your Excellency in the hope that it may at least ameliorate the trouble I have put you to."

"What treasure?" asked the lord sharply.

The prisoner opened his hand and revealed the peach pit. "This is it, Your Excellency."

The lord laughed. "That is nothing but a worthless seed. You must be trying to insult this court!"

"No, Your Excellency," said the prisoner humbly. "In my career as a thief I stole this peach pit from the treasure chest of a sorcerer. This seed has magical qualities."

"What qualities?" asked the lord, a look of interest appearing on his face.

"When planted at the full of the moon this seed grows into a tree that yields peaches of the purest gold," said the prisoner, holding the seed toward the lord.

"The why didn't you plant it" asked the lord shrewdly. "You would not then have had to steal."

"I intended to, Your Excellency. But then I learned that the seed will only bear fruit if the person who plants it is free of crimes." He paused. "That is why I thought of you. No person in your position could be guilty of dishonesty."

The lord reached for the seed and then paused. His expression changed and he withdrew his hand. "I, er...I have no use of further wealth," he said. "But perhaps my able secretary here," he indicated the deputy to his left, "…My secretary, who keeps a faithful record of all that happens in my domain, might better use such a seed."

The secretary looked flustered. "But I couldn't possibly accept such a treasure, Your Excellency. Perhaps my honourable colleague, the treasurer, who guards Your Excellency's wealth with such vigour, might be a better recipient."

The treasurer drew back as if from a serpent. "Oh, no, I couldn't…" he said, and squirmed as the eye of the lord rested on him. "Maybe one of Your Excellency's other loyal servants…" his voice trailed off.

There was silence. Finally the lord spoke. "I have heard that you are a clever man, Thief," he said. "But I did not expect a lesson this morning. I will now adjourn this tribunal while I have a word with my loyal deputies." He turned his gaze on both of the men, who were busily examining nothing in particular.

"It seems that no one is entirely free of guilt," he said, and banged his gavel. "Court dismissed. Oh, and as for you, Thief—or should I call you Professor? You are free to go."

The old man stroked the peach seed as he finished his tale. His young visitor asked a question with his eyes.

"Instead of a ring, my wife wore this poor locket around her neck all the days of her life," said the old man. "That is why I wear it now, and why I say it reminds me daily of who I am."

Dishing the Dirt

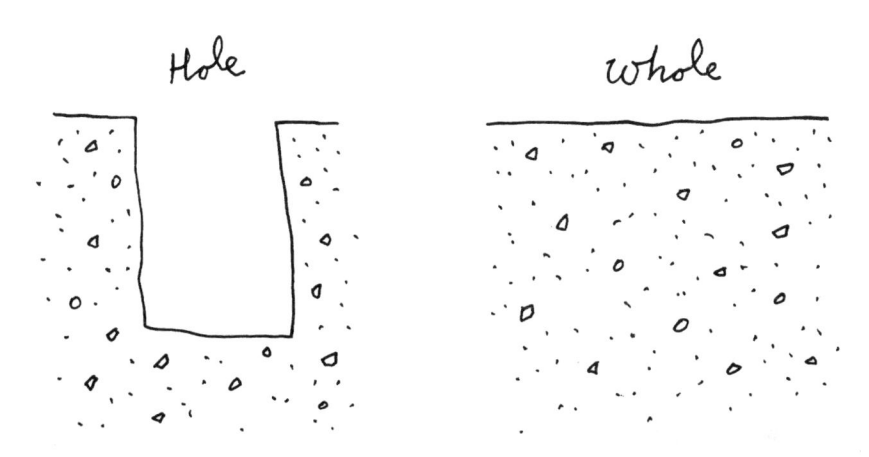

Hole   whole

A boy was getting teased and insulted by others at school. He tried and tried to get them to stop, but it continued until he was feeling desperate. He told his parents, but they just said it would pass and not to worry.

One day he was walking past a tree where a very old man sat. This old man was thought to be a holy man, and the boy was nervous of him and tried to pass by quickly. As he hurried along, the old man whistled. The boy saw he was being summoned.

"Why are you looking so sad?" asked the holy man.

"The other boys all call me names," the boy said, and before he knew it, he was telling the old man his problem. The holy man nodded gravely as the boy spoke.

When he had finished, he said, "Come and take a walk with me." He picked up his walking stick and rose very slowly and the two started off down a country lane.

They walked for quite a while in silence. As they rounded a bend, they saw a group of men huddled around what seemed to be a broken wooden platform.

"Have you got your donkey out of the well yet?" the old man asked one of the fellows.

"No," said a worried-looking farmer. "We keep trying to put a rope around him, but he just kicks it away and ignores us."

The boy peered over the edge and saw a small donkey standing in the dark twelve feet down. It was clear what had happened; the donkey had stood on the rotten platform and made it collapse.

"Lucky for you it's a dry well," said one of the men. "Or the beast would have drowned."

The donkey's owner looked at the holy man. "Master," can you tell me how to get the donkey out of there?"

"Throw dirt on him," said the holy man. He went and sat in the shade of a nearby tree.

"What good will that do?" the farmer asked. "The animal will just stand there until he's buried completely." But the old man said nothing, and in desperation the men began shovelling dirt into the well. The donkey ignored them, but shook off all the soil as it landed and kicked it away with a hoof. The boy joined the old man under the tree.

"Does that remind you of anything?" asked the old man.

"What do you mean?" asked the boy. But the old man said nothing. They sat and watched as the sweating men dumped dirt into the well.

At length one of the men shouted, "He's climbing out!" The donkey took a step each time a load of dirt landed on the floor of the well, and within an hour had risen enough to put his hooves over the lip of the well. The men reached down and dragged him out. The donkey was dirty but apparently unbothered. He started grazing the weeds of the verge immediately. The old man rose and the boy followed.

"I think I know what you meant," he said to the holy man. "The other boys are throwing dirt on me, but if I kick it away, I will be able to lift myself with it."

"That well needed filling, anyway," said the old man.

Less is More

Once upon a time, when people still lived in caves, a man who had travelled far in his youth returned to his home village, bringing many things along with him. One of these was a cart that he could pull behind him and carry things that were too heavy for his arms. It was not so long after the wheel had been invented, and everyone was amazed at how much he could carry. They were jealous, too, because no one really understood how it worked. The man would walk whistling past other people carrying loads of logs and stones, and they would just shake their heads in wonder.

The only problem was that roads hadn't been invented yet, and so the cart would rattle and shake on the rough ground and make a terrible racket. Then one day something terrible happened: a front wheel broke into pieces, making the cart useless. It would just drag on the ground when pulled, making the work even harder. Making a new one was out of the question, and no one had any ideas of what to do. So he put the cart in front of his cave door and used it to piles things in, things like old animal bones and pieces of flint he couldn't make into blades.

Years passed. People became so used to seeing the cart parked there that they stopped noticing. But one young boy was fascinated with it. He would touch the wheels with his hands and imagine them turning, rolling along the ground, loaded with good things from too far away to carry. The owner of the cart chased him away, but soon tired of this.

"Listen," he said one day. "I'm tired of always seeing you outside my door. If I give you that useless thing, will you promise to go and not come back?"

The boy cheerfully agreed, and the same day dragged the useless cart home. His parents scolded him. What was he doing with that silly thing, they wanted to know.

"I'm fixing it," said the boy, and began to work.

"Then why are you taking two more wheels off?"

"Some things work better when there's less of it," he said.

The following morning, people awoke to the sound of whistling. They looked out to see the boy pushing—not pulling – the cart, loaded with a great heap of firewood. They stared in amazement at this boy genius who had repaired the cart by removing wheels and inventing the wheelbarrow.

The Dirtiest Face

A spiritual teacher was asked by the headmaster of a local boys' school to come and give a talk to the students. Most of the pupils were well-behaved, and sat quietly while the teacher talked about the spiritual path, virtue and seeking truth. One boy, however, was disruptive. He made faces at the other boys, threw spit balls and made animal noises.

The teacher stopped his lecture and looked at the boy, who shrank lower in his seat.

"Come up here, my son," the teacher said.

The boy came up onto the dais reluctantly. The spiritual teacher asked him his name, but the boy just shrugged and made faces. Nevertheless, the teacher treated him with great warmth, tousled his hair and reached into his bag and handed the boy an apple. He munched happily, rolling his eyes at the other boys, who squirmed with embarrassment. He was held next to the teacher throughout the lecture. Afterwards, the spiritual teacher thanked the boy and sent him back to his seat.

After the program the headmaster apologised for the behaviour of the boy. "He is always like that," he sighed. "Some boys are just born trouble-makers."

"But he is an excellent child," said the spiritual teacher. "The best of the whole group."

"But he was rude and disruptive!" said the headmaster, astonished. "Why would you say he was the best?"

"I will let you answer that yourself after hearing a little story," said the teacher. "Two firemen are called out to a burning house. They enter the building and manage to put out the fire. Afterwards they meet at their fire engine and look at each other.

"One of them has a face blackened with soot and ash. The other's face is clean." He paused. "Which one goes to wash his face?"

"Why the one with the soot and ash on his face," said the headmaster. "Of course."

The teacher was silent. Knowing of the wise man's reputation for unexpected answers, the headmaster thought for a moment more.

"No," he said at last. "I see! The one with the clean face will assume that his is dirty too, since he cannot see it. So his face will become doubly clean."

The teacher smiled. "Which one has done the others the best favour?" he asked.

Spooning out the Lake

An energetic pilgrim seeking enlightenment travelled to see a well-known spiritual teacher who lived by the shores of a lake. When the pilgrim arrived, he was surprised to find the master sitting on a rock with a fishing pole. He had expected to see him engaged in teaching and preaching right and wrong. Nevertheless, he explained that he had come to learn how to eliminate evil in the world.

"Why does that interest you?" asked the master.

"Because the world is full of poor behaviour and mistaken ideas," said the pilgrim.

"And you wish to change this?" asked the master.

"I do."

The master stood and told the pilgrim to follow him. They walked for a few miles in silence through the forest until they got to the shores of a small lake—a large pond, really.

"Build your hut here," said the master. He reached into his pocket and pulled out a spoon. "Using this tool, spoon out the waters of this pond until it is dry. You will then achieve your goal."

The pilgrim was taken aback. The task the master wanted him to accomplish was huge! But, being a dedicated seeker, he agreed to follow the master's instructions. After building himself a shelter, he began spooning out the waters of the lake.

Months passed, and then years. When it rained, it seemed that all his work was being undone. But, thanks to two years of drought, he finally succeeded.

One day the master was walking through the forest when he came upon the much older pilgrim sitting quietly in front of a pond he had never seen before. He was sitting on a rock with a fishing pole. He seemed much more relaxed and cheerful than the young man with his burning eyes who had come all those years ago.

"I see you have attained your goal," the master said.

"Yes," said the pilgrim. "After beginning my task, I soon realised that if I removed the water from the lake that I would need someplace else to put it." He waved his hand at the new lake he had created.

"How is the fishing?" asked the master, and sat down to join him.

The Doctor of Unicorns

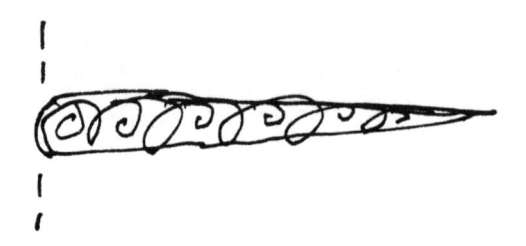

A young girl was travelling in a car with her parents. The father took a short cut along a country road. From her window she saw a field with ponies grazing. One of them had a big spiralled horn growing from his forehead. Just then a man ran toward the pony and led it away to a barn, with a furtive look over his shoulder at the car, which contained the only witnesses.

The girl asked her parents to stop and turn around, because she had seen something amazing. But they merely laughed. Do you know what a pony with a horn would be called? Her father asked. It would be a unicorn, and unicorns don't exist.

"But I saw what I saw," said the girl.

Many years later, the girl was travelling in the same neighbourhood. She had never forgotten what she had seen, or thought she had seen, from the car. On impulse, she turned off onto a back road, looking for the same farm. After a few minutes she spotted what seemed to be the same field. There were ponies grazing, but none of them had horns.

At last the woman was close to convincing herself that she had merely imagined the glimpse of the unicorn. She turned around in the farm's driveway, and saw a man in her rear view mirror. She couldn't be sure, but he looked to be the very same man she had seen, despite looking older. On impulse, she parked the car and approached the man.

She explained that she was following up her childhood memory and laughed nervously. The man looked at her for a moment as if making a decision, and then said, "You are at the right place. I am the doctor of unicorns."

She followed him into his barn. He opened a door and she saw inside stacks of magnificent horns. She gasped. "You turn these marvellous creatures into ordinary ponies? Why would you do something like that?" The doctor of unicorns led her to where a pony was peacefully standing, half-asleep in a stall. He put his hand gently on the pony's flank and showed her the place where the horn had stood, now nearly covered with hair.

"What do you think would happen if word got out that there really were unicorns?"

"It would be amazing. A news sensation!"

"And then what would happen to these animals? They would be sold for fabulous sums, become the property of investors and rich hobbyists. They would be flown to places like Arabia. They would be poked and prodded, x-rayed and genetically tested. They would never be free to run in the open air again. That is why I help them by removing their horns."

At first the young woman protested. Then, through an open door she watched the ponies grazing happily in the field.

"I understand," she said. "Sometimes it is better to be happy than to be famous."

"I would say we are preventing the world from destroying a lovely myth," the Doctor of Unicorns said.

Poverty is Expensive

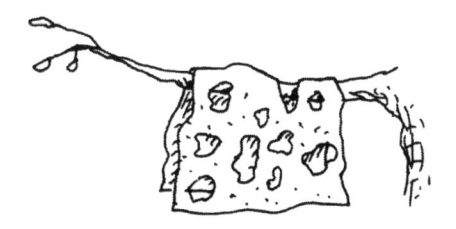

A serious young man from a prosperous family decided to leave behind all thoughts of worldly pleasures and success and devote himself to the search for enlightenment. Knowing that the spiritual path was full of twists and turns, he decided to consult a well-known sage for advice before beginning his search.

The old man received the seeker politely, although there seemed to be a glint of amusement in his eye as he listened to the young man's request.

At last he said, "The path begins with poverty. The best thing to do is to live simply, wearing only a loincloth."

That same day the young man left his weeping family wearing only a dhoti, the loincloth favoured by sadhus and sanyassins from time immemorial. He went to a patch of forest belonging to his family, built himself a rough shelter of branches, and lay down on a bed of leaves and grass. Before retiring, being a clean young man, he washed the dhoti and hung it over a limb to dry.

In the morning he awoke full of enthusiasm for the spiritual search. He went out to get his loincloth and found that rats had eaten holes in it during the night. He repaired it as best he could and put it on. He spent the rest of the day in meditation, eating berries and nuts from the forest and drinking water from the river. That night he hung the dhoti from a higher limb and turned in satisfied with his progress.

In the morning, however, there were still more rat holes in his dhoti. During the day, thoughts of the dhoti interrupted his meditation. As he went to bed that night, less satisfied with his progress, he had an idea. It was simple to solve the rat problem: he would get a cat.

So the following day he went into town and found one of the many stray cats roaming the streets for scraps of food. He took it back to the forest, and retired. In the morning he saw with satisfaction that the rats had not eaten his dhoti. But soon a new problem appeared; the cat was mewing with hunger.

He went into town again and begged a bowl of milk to feed to the cat. This went on for several days, keeping him from his meditation. Finally, a neighbour advised him to buy a cow. With a cow to provide milk, the cat would never go hungry. He went home to his family's home and borrowed money from his father, who was pleased to see him again. He bought a cow, a small brown one, from the first farmer he saw and led her home.

The following morning the cow gave plenty of milk, enough to satisfy him and the cat. But there was a new problem: the cow was lowing with hunger because there was no cleared land in which to graze.

That problem, too, had a remedy. The young man borrowed an axe and hoe, and began to clear the forest. Soon the new grass shot up, and the cow was satisfied. But weeds began to grow in the new pasture. He thought and thought about this new problem, forgetting to meditate. He soon realised that he would need to employ a few men to help. Before long there were six labourers at work, and, because they needed to be paid and fed, the young man bought more cattle and began to sell his milk in the village.

He had become too busy to spend much time in meditation. Finally a solution occurred to him. He would get married, and his wife could help by looking after the affairs of the farm, leaving him free to meditate and find enlightenment.

So he married and brought his wife back to his hut in the forest. But she was unhappy with the poor accommodation, so he had a large house erected. Not long after that, his first child was born.

One day the young man looked up from his ledger books to see a familiar face at the window. It was the old sage. The look of amusement had not left his face.

"I came by to see how you were getting on with the spiritual search," he said, without a trace of irony.

The young man sighed. "I've had to abandon it for a while," he said ruefully. "Being poor is just too expensive."

The Seeker's Dilemma

A seeker had spent all his adult life searching for God. He could usually be seen sitting on the steps of the cathedral in the crowded main square of the city, dressed in rags and with a long, scraggly beard. People gave him food and water, but no one knew where he slept. Everyone who passed was asked the same question, "Do you know where I can find God?"

Of course, no one did.

One day he was at his usual spot when a neatly dressed man in a business suit walked up. "Do you know where I can find God?" asked the seeker.

"Why, yes I do," said the man. "I happen to be an angel, and I have come to give you God's street address."

"Oh glory be!" shouted the seeker. The man handed him a small business card and disappeared into the crowd. Or disappeared somewhere, anyway.

The seeker wasted no time. He began to shout: "I've found Him, I've found Him!" people turned and stared as he hurried through the market. He went down broad avenues, passed parks and stadiums, turned into small side streets, went past houses made of bricks and houses made of wood and at last found a tiny cottage, all white, with no window, just a door. Hesitating, he knocked.

"Yes?" said a deep voice from within.

"I'm looking for God," said the seeker in a hushed voice.

"You've found Me," came the reply. "Come in, my child."

An hour later he was back in the town square, sitting on the steps of the cathedral. As people passed, he asked his usual question: "Do you know where I can find God?"

A bystander approached him and said, "You're back? I thought you had found God."

"I did," said the seeker. "I know where He lives."

"Then why do you continue to search?" asked the puzzled bystander.

"Then what would I do all day?" said the seeker.

The Horse Might Talk

Of course I can't talk!

There was a certain court jester, whose job it was, by long tradition, to poke fun at the king and thereby keep him alert to the realities of life outside the splendid walls of his palace. Because of his privileged position, he alone could risk getting too personal with His Majesty's affairs, his appearance, even the fact that he snored loudly at night. One day, however, he went too far, and accused the king of excessive flatulence.

The king became enraged. At the urging of his ministers, he resolved to punish the jester. The following day the jester was in the royal courtyard when the king rode up on his horse, accompanied by a squad of cavalry. He pointed to the jester and ordered his soldiers to put him to death.

The jester said, "Sire, of course you have every right to order my execution, but there is just one thing I'd like you to consider. If you have me killed, then I will not be able to teach your horse to talk."

The king was startled. How can you teach a beast to

speak?" he scoffed. "Are you actually claiming that you can teach my horse to talk like a person?"

"Certainly, your majesty," replied the jester. "If you give me one year to comply, I will do so."

The king thought for a moment. Then he said, "All right then. I will spare your life for one year, but at the end of that time, if the horse can't talk, I will have you killed." He rode away, not looking back.

A bystander came over and said, "Now what are you going to do?"

The jester just smiled. He said, "In one year the king might die, I might die, or the horse might talk."

From a story told by Gilly Fraser

Survival of the Fittest

cuT

MINE / YouRS

Great-uncle Silas had finally died in bed after many years of travelling the world, exploring unknown regions and acquiring a fortune. His ruthlessness as a businessman was legendary, but for the last thirty years of his life he lived alone in a 19th century mansion on a hill overlooking the sea.

His only relatives were a pair of brothers, who had never actually met the old man, though they, like everyone else, had heard the stories. They hardly dared hope for it, but at last each received a registered letter from Uncle Silas' butler. They were asked to attend a special meeting at the dead man's home, in which the attorney and executor would read the will.

For many years the brothers had not been on speaking terms. Reginald, the elder brother, lived in California. He had owned and lost a succession of business ventures and now worked as a salesman of camping caravans. Roderick was a teacher in a city several hundred miles away. He had been married to the same woman for twenty years. He drove the long journey in his seven-year-old estate car, arriving at the imposing house just in time to see his brother pull up in a rented Mercedes. Their greeting was strained, even after so many years, and they wasted no time entering the mansion.

A butler met them cordially and showed them into an ornate library where the lawyer sat behind a old-fashioned desk the size of a ping pong table. He was a busy-looking man with pearl cufflinks and thick glasses. After seating the two brothers, the butler left.

"Time is short, gentlemen, so I will get right to the point. Having read the will of your late great-uncle, I can attest to the fact that the estate, after liquidation of real property and inheritance taxes, amounts to approximately 162 million pounds."

The brothers gasped. "Who inherits it," asked Reg immediately.

The lawyer cleared his throat. "This is highly irregular," he said, "The beneficiary is to be one of you two. Only one, I'm afraid. But this might create certain legal entanglements. You see, the inheritance will go to whichever of you is surviving on a certain date in the future. There is no provision whatever for the case in which both of you are alive."

"When is the date?" asked Reg.

The lawyer removed his glasses and polished them with a handkerchief before answering. "Tomorrow," he said.

There was a collective gasp. The butler entered, carrying a tray with two glasses. Inside was a hot, pleasant-tasting but exotic tea. Reg gulped his down like a shot of whiskey and Rod sipped his slowly.

The shock was just beginning to fade when the lawyer announced, "The will also stipulates that I read out the following." He slit open a letter with a red wax seal.

"To my esteemed grand nephews," the attorney read. He faltered, then continued. "You have both just consumed a deadly poison which I have carefully guarded from my travels in Southeast Asia. The toxin is not fast-acting. However, without intervention in the form of an antidote, you will both die within several hours."

Rod, who had just finished his drink, dropped the glass onto the floor. The lawyer continued reading, his face as white as the paper he was holding.

"The antidote is in the form of a tablet, and that tablet lies now within your sight." All three men looked around the room quickly. Reg leaned forward, his knuckles white on the arms of the chair. Rod simply looked dazed.

"And the last paragraph," continued the lawyer "Says that there is absolutely no point in calling for medical help. The poison is unknown to Western medicine, and, in any case, you will almost certainly die before an ambulance can arrive." Reg replaced the mobile phone he had yanked from his pocket.

"I have done this," continued the letter, "To establish and demonstrate one eternal fact. Survival belongs to the fittest. The weak and the unwary are not destined to survive."

The lawyer looked up. "Your uncle was a hard man, gentlemen. An old-fashioned man in many ways. But this is barbaric. He has actually managed to commit murder after his own death."

"It won't be murder if we find the pills," said Reg. "Let's get on it. Is that all it says?"

The lawyer looked at him gravely. Rod had already anticipated his next words and sat with his head in his hands.

"There's only one, Reg," he said. "One tablet and two dying men."

The lawyer made an apology and nearly ran to the door. "I'll call for…assistance, gentlemen," he said over his shoulder as he left. "Good… good luck."

Reg kicked his chair over, swearing. He looked around wildly, went to the mantelpiece and began to empty flower vases, ashtrays and an ornate wooden chest. Rod sat still for a moment. On the desk, under the brass lamp, he spotted a small brown envelope. Leaning forward, he picked it up and tore open the sealed end. Inside was a single white tablet, scored with a line which dissected it. He sat back for a moment and watched his older brother ravage the antiques while the butler looked on sourly from the door.

"I have it, Reg," Rod said.

His brother wheeled. "Let me see it!" he yelled. Rod sat with his palm open.

"It's evident what we have to do, Reg," he said. "We'll have to share this. Each of us will take half, and hope that the antidote is strong enough to keep us from dying, even though we'll almost certainly be very ill."

"You're right, of course," Reg said. "Here, I'll break it." He grabbed the tablet from Rod's hand, held it an arm's length away for a moment, muttered, "Sorry," and swallowed it whole. The butler made no move. Rod's head fell into his hands. "I guess you're the fittest all right, brother," he said. "I couldn't do that to you."

"You do what you have to," said Reg. He started pacing the room "Just in time, because I think I can feel the poison coming on already." His face turned red and foam began flecking his lips. "In fact, I…" He made a strangled sound and fell to his knees before toppling over onto the carpet. Rod rushed to his side, but the butler intervened.

"It will be too late," he said. "The tablet acts very quickly."

"The tablet? But that's the antidote, isn't it?"

"Perhaps I should read this letter now," said the butler, tearing open an identical envelope to the one opened by the lawyer.

"By now one of you is dead," came the stark words of his great-uncle. "The tablet is a fast acting form of the toxin I described in the earlier letter. An entire pill is enough to kill a man, but half of that dose would give an attack of stomach cramps and a severe headache, and would not prove fatal to a healthy person. Had you divided the tablet, you would have assumed that you were experiencing the effects of the tea you consumed earlier, and you would both have recovered. In that event, you would not now be hearing these words, but the words of a second letter also entrusted to my servant, which provides a codicil to my will to the effect that the money from my estate would have been divided between you."

The butler paused and removed a third envelope from his breast pocket, which he threw into the fire.

"I have been known as a calculating man, some would say a hard one. My life has been a case of the very maxim 'survival of the fittest'. But times have changed, and so has the meaning of those words. What now constitutes the fittest is the person most likely to share resources, whose first reaction is to co-operate, not compete. Whether that has been proved here today, I shall never know."

"Nor will Reginald," Rod said softly.

I'm out Here

There was once a very devout woman named Mary. She was so devout that she prayed all the time. She counted her rosary while she worked and said hundreds of prayers every day. Her goal in life was to hear from God, and that was what she prayed, over and over.

Every afternoon she went to the parish church to light a candle and she spent the hours with her head bowed. On her way there and her way home she didn't look left or right, never stopped to notice the people in the street. She passed by children playing, beggars begging and sick patients queued up outside the doors of the charity hospital. She didn't blink when a hearse drove past or when someone tried to speak to her. She ignored drunks and dogs and friendly old ladies. Her life's goal was fixed and she was determined.

One night she had a dream. It seemed to be a great cloud that swirled overhead. It seemed to her that she could see a word formed by the shape of the cloud. The word was "tomorrow". So when she woke up she was delighted. Today she would hear from God! So she got up and rushed out of her house, looking neither left nor right, ignoring dogs and drunks and sick people and friendly old ladies.

When she reached the doors of the church she was startled to find that it was locked. She looked around for a priest or someone to let her in, feeling more and more desperate. She didn't even notice the ragged old tramp sitting on the steps.

"Are you called Mary?" the tramp asked.

Mary ignored him. She continued to try the door. There must be some mistake! Today was the day she would hear from God.

"Because, if you are," the tramp said, "I have a message for you from God."

Mary nearly laughed. "What do you know about God?" she asked harshly.

"Not a lot," said the tramp. "But He was just here and told me to give a message to someone named Mary."

Stunned, Mary turned to look at him for the first time. Could it be?

"What was the message?" she asked querulously.

"He said to tell you that He's out here," the tramp replied.

Two Ways to Become Rich

RICH MAN   POOR MAN

The rabbi was widely respected for his wisdom, and many people, both Jew and Gentile, came to ask for his advice. The community was poor, and most of people's problems, in one way or another, came down to not having enough money. Since there was no way to ensure that people would be able to acquire the riches they sought, the rabbi spent many hours trying to find other ways to help.

After much prayer, he managed to make contact with an angel. The angel, like the rabbi, was desperately overworked, and so their meeting was brief. When the rabbi asked for help solving the financial problems of his poor neighbours, the angel said enigmatically. "Show them that there are two ways to become rich."

The rabbi thought about these words for hours. He turned over possibilities in his mind, but could not understand the meaning of the words. He decided to contact the overworked angel again, as soon as possible, and get an explanation.

The next day a poor farmer knocked on the rabbi's door. He held his hat in his hands and told the rabbi an all too familiar tale.

"My family is large, Rabbi," he said. It seems that every year my wife gives birth. And our house is so small there is hardly room for us all to move about."

The rabbi clucked his tongue in sympathy and let the man continue, though he could probably have finished the man's story for him. They earned little money, the children ate like ravening wolves and all they possessed was a little livestock: a goat, a cow and six hens. They would never be able to afford a larger house.

Thinking over the angel's statement, the rabbi had an idea.

"I think I can help you," he said. What you must do is take your livestock out of their barn and move them into the house with you."

"But, Rabbi…"

"There is more than one way to become rich," the rabbi said.

A week later there was another knock on the door. The farmer had even more complaints.

"Whatever you had in mind, it's not working! Things are ten times worse now, with the animals inside the house, Rabbi," he moaned. "Now there really is no room to turn around. And the smell…"

"There is more than one way to become rich," was all the rabbi had to say, as he showed the farmer out.

Another week passed, but the farmer didn't return. The rabbi took a walk by the man's farm. He found the farmer whistling cheerfully in front of his house. His wife smiled at him from the door.

"Have you discovered the other way to become rich?" asked the rabbi.

"Rabbi, you were so right! As soon as I decided to put the animals back in the barn, things got better right away. There is now so much space for us that we all feel as if we had made the house bigger."

There was no need to ask the angel what the words meant, the rabbi mused on his way home. The second way to become rich is to become satisfied with what you have.

The Tiger's Whisker

After the war was over, the men who had survived came home. But they were not the same as before. Shanti's husband had been gone for no longer than a year, but for many months, although his body was there before her, his mind was somewhere else. She could not communicate with him. He sat silently through the days, hardly bothering to help tend the crops, his eyes as vacant and cold as those of a stranger.

She knew that he had seen terrible things, things he could not forget. And she knew that if anyone was to reach him, it would be up to her. She cooked him her best scented rice, flavoured delicately with herbs from the forest, which he ate indifferently, sometimes leaving his bowl half full, even though her rice was famous in the village.

She consulted other women. They had no suggestions.

When she asked the priest, he simply advised her to pray. This she did, bowed for hours on her mat, while her husband lay sleepless beside her. But no sign came from the gods.

One day a friend told her of a certain hermit that lived high in a pass in the mountains that ringed the village. He was rarely seen, but people told stories of his wisdom. She determined to ask the hermit's advice. She was, she felt, ready to try anything.

The following morning she rose with the dawn and began the trek up the narrow path, past the waterfall, across a slippery rock face, through a dense forest, and finally reached the pass. In the clearing she saw a cave with a narrow entrance. Inside, there seemed to be a dim light. Gathering her courage, she went in and saw a small bent man sitting in front of a small fire.

Without turning to face her, the hermit said, "Come in, my child."

Shanti approached cautiously. The man was bald and clothed in a simple brown robe. She could not determine his age, but when he turned his eyes on her she felt as if she were looking into centuries past, as if the hermit had sat here for lifetimes come and gone.

"What can I help you with?" came his voice. It was coarse with disuse, but not unkind.

Shanti explained about her husband. Her words came out in such a rush that they tumbled over each other. When she had finished, there was silence. The hermit's eyes had never left her face.

"I suppose you are seeking some sort of potion that will heal your husband's heart?"

"Yes. Something that will restore him to me," she said.

After a moment, the hermit said, "Such a medicine does exist. I can make it for you. I have all the necessary ingredients to hand." He paused. "Except one."

"What is it, Master? Surely I can find it somewhere and bring it to you," said Shanti excitedly. "I know most of the herbs of the forest."

"This is no ordinary ingredient," replied the hermit. "What we will need is the whisker of a tiger. And it must be plucked from the beast's head while he lives."

Shanti's heart fell. "But that's impossible!" she cried. "How can I pluck a whisker from a tiger without dying? I am weak. I am afraid. And I am just a woman."

"Nevertheless that is what is required," said the hermit. His expression had not changed. "You must do this in order to heal the heart of your beloved."

All the way back down the mountain path, Shanti turned his words over and over in her mind. No one could take a whisker from a ferocious animal and survive. Least of all a woman! She had never felt weaker or more helpless. But by the time she reached her home, she was beginning, impossible though it seemed, to plan.

The next morning she awoke and immediately lit the cooking fire in the hearth. While the water was heating, she carefully examined each grain of rice from her large bag, selecting only the finest grains. She plucked fresh herbs from the edge of the forest and begged a pan of fish heads from a neighbour to make a broth. Skilfully, with all her attention, she made what she knew was the most flavoursome pot of rice in her life. Her husband showed no interest, but she didn't stop working until she was finished.

The sun was already beginning to dip in the sky when she began her trek up the mountain, along the narrow path, beside the waterfall, across the slippery rock face, through the forest, through the clearing of the hermit's cave and on up and up to beyond the tree line, where she knew the tigers had their lairs. By the time she reached the plateau, she was exhausted, and the light was beginning to fail. The ground was strewn with the bones of animals slaughtered by the tiger, and a chill shook her as she thought that some of them might even be human. At the far end of the plateau was a cave. She knew that this must be the home of the beast she sought.

Feeling that inhuman eyes were watching her, she carefully unwrapped the parcel she was carrying, a bowl made of woven banana leaves. As she uncovered it, the delicious smell of the food rose around her. Suddenly gripped by panic, she placed the bowl on the ground and ran. She retraced her steps and went lurching through half- darkness all the way back to her home. Her husband hardly seemed to notice.

The following morning she did the same thing all over again. This pot of rice was, if anything, even more delicious.

Her trek began again, but now she was more accustomed to the trail. As she passed the cave of the hermit, she thought she could feel his ancient eyes on her.

At the plateau she found the bowl of rice from the day before. Every single grain had been eaten. With slightly more light this time, she dared to look for a moment at the cave's entrance. She thought she saw something gleaming in the darkness of the lair. Could it be a pair of non-human eyes, sizing her up for a meal? She returned home, but this time she did not run.

So began many weeks of taking food for the tiger. She became stronger and less fearful. Sometimes she called out to the hermit as she passed his cave, though there was never any response. Each day was the same. The bowl of the day before was lying empty among the bones. She began to expect the same routine, which was why she was surprised one day to see a fully grown male tiger, lying indolently at the cave's mouth, twitching his tail.

Her first reaction was shock and she resisted an impulse to run crying from the plateau. But she forced herself to stand still and look back at the huge animal. Their eyes met for a moment. Shanti turned slowly and began her descent, feeling that something had somehow changed, though she could not say what.

Thereafter, each afternoon when she arrived, the tiger was there. Sometimes he seemed to be sleeping. At other times he was playing with a stone or a stick with his enormous paw.

He seemed just like a huge house cat. Her fear decreased with each visit, and she shocked herself by one day holding the rice bowl out to the animal as you would with a shy house pet. The tiger would approach slowly, but never quite reach her outstretched hands.

One morning she awoke and knew the day had arrived. Feeling stronger than she could remember, she nearly bounded up the trail which had now become as familiar as her own garden. This time the tiger stood at the entrance to the plateau. His eyes, focussed in her, seemed no more frightening than the eyes of a child. She heard herself calling to him in a soothing voice, as to a child. The tiger came all the way forward and then rolled over playfully onto his back, as if he wanted his belly scratched.

Shanti leaned forward and touched the thick fur of the tiger's head. Half expecting him to purr, she reached out with her other hand and took hold of one of the thick whiskers. "Forgive me, Mr Tiger, for what I must do," she whispered, and yanked sharply, pulling a whisker free. The tiger didn't seem to notice. Shanti left his bowl of rice and turned away. A feeling of something like sadness rose in her breast. "Thank you," she whispered as she walked away. "Thank you for saving my husband."

She nearly ran to the cave of the hermit. "Master!" she called out as she entered his cave." I have it! I have the whisker of a living tiger!"

"So you have, my child," said the hermit, without rising

from his seat by the fire. He took it in his fingers and held it up to the light. It seemed to glow in his hand. Then, in a single motion, he dropped it into the fire.

Shanti cried out, "But you have destroyed it!" A flood of tears threatened to overwhelm her. "Now how can I save my husband?"

The hermit replied calmly, "When I first told you what you needed to do, what did you say?"

"I said that I was weak. That I was merely a woman and incapable of doing what you asked."

"And now?" asked the hermit.

"I am more capable than I thought," said Shanti "I am not weak. I am patient. I am strong. I am even brave."

She thought she saw the briefest of smiles flicker across the hermits face.

"Is the heart of a man more terrible than the teeth of a tiger?" he replied gently.

From a Korean folk tale, heard re-told by Michael Meade
with the aid of a drum.

The Seeds

The king was growing old and knew he would not live very long. He had a son to take his place, but the boy was too young to govern by himself. He feared that the kingdom might not prosper. He decided to appoint an advisor from among the courtiers who surrounded him.

He called three of them together and explained that he was looking for a worthy advisor to his son after he had passed away. He handed each of them a tiny seed, told them to go away and grow the seed and return in six months to show him what had grown.

When they returned six months later, the king asked them to show him the results of their efforts. Two of them showed him pots in which a healthy plant had grown, each bearing flowers.

"Lovely!" said the king. "But what of your seed?" he asked the third man.

The fellow sadly showed what he had been holding behind his back—a flower pot empty except for the soil. "I'm afraid I have failed, your Majesty," he said.

"On the contrary," said the king. "You will advise my son."

Later the boy asked his father why he had chosen the failure to advise him.

"The two who brought healthy plants were both cheats. I gave all three seeds which I had boiled. They were dead, and could not grow. But one of them is an honest man. He is the best one to advise a king."

The Parrot Who Made It Rain

Once upon a time in a forest, animals and birds lived together in harmony, each getting on with their own lives, until one day a small fire started in a corner of the wood. The flames spread quickly, and the animals began to flee from the fire until they were crowded together at the edge of a cliff so steep that no one could scale it.

The birds were able to fly over the fire, out of danger. But from the sky they could hear the cries of terror as all the others massed against the cliff: foxes with rabbits, snakes with hedgehogs-- all in danger of being destroyed.

A parrot, flying alone overhead, suddenly dipped and dived into the river carrying on his wings a few drops of water, which he shook out over the raging flames. The drops disappeared without trace into the blaze, but the parrot continued undaunted, swooping again and again into the water.

After a while, an eagle flew up alongside the parrot and said, "What you are doing is silly, Parrot. Those few drops can make no difference against such a large fire."

The parrot answered, "I thought you eagles were brave. What's the matter, are you frightened?" The eagle, never to be outdared, swooped wordlessly into the river, and the drops from those great wings carried even more water, which were added to the parrot's.

In a moment, an owl flew alongside and said, "Parrot, it is obvious that the strength of the flames will outstrip any effort you might make to quench them."

The parrot responded, "Owl, you are wiser than I, but even you must see that this little is better than nothing at all." Ever logical, the owl joined the parrot and the eagle in their swooping, and then there were three.

Seeing that the wisest and bravest of birds had joined the parrot, the leader of the sparrows said to the sparrow multitudes, "Let us join in, because the wisest and bravest must know what they are doing."

And so they did, and in their thousands began to dive and shake loose drops of water into the flames. Soon all the birds of the forest were dipping and diving and shaking drops of water from their wings, and the forest was drenched as if from a mighty rain.

The fire was extinguished, but not the legend of the parrot who made it rain.

Turning Wine into Water

After many years in exile the king was returning to his home. Everyone was very excited, because the king had always ruled with fairness and generosity to all. It was decided that the whole kingdom would come out to greet him with a huge feast worthy of such a personage.

The treasury was nearly exhausted, but the advisors managed to provide an ox to roast, herbs and spices from the decaying gardens of the palace, and ripe fruits from the orchards. Everything was nearly in readiness, when the Grand Vizier made a startling discovery. He had forgotten the wine! As it would be impossible to greet the king properly without the elixir of the vineyards, there was only one thing to do. Everyone must bring a large measure of wine from their own household vats.

Tobin the farmer sighed at this news. His own grapes had not yielded well the previous season, and his household had little to spare. He would be as delighted as anyone to see the king once again on his throne, but wine was so costly!

On the day of the feast, people began arriving in hordes. The head of each household stood in a long queue, and one by one emptied large vessels from their homes into a great common vat. The guards of the Grand Vizier stood sternly by until each householder had complied.

Tobin quickly poured the contents of his vessel into the vat, feeling a great sense of satisfaction. With such quantities being donated, no one would be able to tell that his own contribution was nothing but plain water from his well. He took his place at one of the long tables. When the king appeared, ushered in great pomp to the high table on the dais, serving girls poured the wine into each person's cup. The Grand Vizier pronounced a long-winded toast, and the king, as was customary, raised his golden goblet to his lips. Taking a single sip, his smile disappeared, and he spat onto the table.

Tobin didn't even taste his cup, realising, as did everyone, that they had found a way to turn wine into water.

The Rustlethudbump

A young man wanted to become a member of a religious order of great fame. This community was known for its deep meditation, its service to the local people and its basic good humour. All he had to do was convince the leader of the community that he was ready. He applied to see the master, and after a wait of several weeks was admitted to an interview.

The master looked at him carefully. "You think you are ready to join us, my son?" he asked in a kindly way.

"Yes, I am," replied the candidate. "I have long awaited my chance to join you."

"You have studied the holy books?"

"Yes, Master."

"You have learned to put behind you all the cares of the world?"

"Indeed I have. And I am skilled at meditation."

"And you have learned to control your thoughts?"

"Completely."

"Then there is one thing you must do first," said the master. "It should be no problem for such an earnest young fellow."

"Anything, Master," said the young man happily.

"It is a small thing, really. You must spend the night alone on the mountain with just a blanket. Can you manage that?"

"Of course," said the young man. "Just show me the place and I am ready to begin."

"Then I will ask one of the brothers to lead you up the mountain path. Report to me here tomorrow and tell me how it went." He stood up and the young man started for the door. "Oh, just one word of advice..." said the master. "Try not to think about the rustlethudbump."

"The rustlethudbump? What is that?" asked the young man.

"Oh, it is a very ferocious animal with a terrible temper. It attacks without warning and even seems to enjoy killing people."

The young man froze. "I have never heard of it," he said.

"Nothing to worry about. It mostly lives far away, and, in any case, it is nearly extinct."

"Oh."

"I'm sure you won't give it a second thought."

"No, Master," said the young man softly.

The following morning the master asked his assistant if he had any interviews that day.

"None, Master," said the assistant.

"And the young man who went up the mountain yesterday?"

"He lasted until about ten pm, your holiness. Then the noises made in the dark by the rustlethudbump drove him shrieking past the gate and away."

How not to be a Farmer

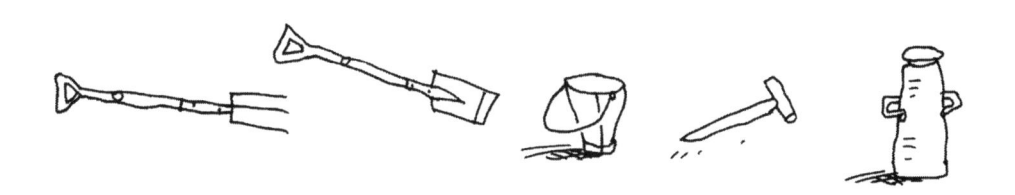

The newlywed son and daughter-in-law of a wealthy merchant decided that they wanted the peace and contentment of the rural life, where they could raise their children under peaceful skies surrounded by the beauty of nature. As a wedding gift, the merchant bought them a small farm in a green valley. Everything a small farmer could need was already there: two cows, a sturdy mule, a few pigs and chickens and a substantial acreage of arable land. There were tools and pens and a snug barn.

Soon after the happy couple moved into their dream home, the merchant began to worry. "My son has no experience in farming," he thought. "He will surely fail unless I do something." He wrote to an old friend, who had been a successful farmer before becoming a professor of agricultural science at the university. His friend had recently retired, and the merchant thought perhaps he could be convinced to help the young couple, by teaching them how to farm.

One day the professor arrived unannounced at the farm gate. He told the young man that he was a retired farmer looking for a bed and board in exchange for his work. The couple welcomed him and gave him a nice bedroom overlooking a pond. They were relieved that someone more experienced than they would be able to give them advice.

Early on the first morning, the professor decided to have a closer look at the farm. At the entrance to the fields he saw the young wife walking with a bucket. He asked where she was going. "To the meadow, to milk the cows," she replied.

"No, no," said the professor impatiently. "You must milk them in the barn before letting them out. Watch me," he said. He got the cows and led them back to the barn and milked them. The bucket was full and the wife was grateful.

A little later the professor came upon the young husband standing by the chicken coop. The birds were scratching in the meadow grass and some had roosted under bushes. "What are you doing?" asked the professor.

"I'm letting the birds run free," said the young man proudly. "They're bound to find their own food and save me some money."

"The foxes will get them and they'll lay their eggs in bramble bushes," said the professor, slapping his head. "Go do something else, and I'll sort out the chickens."

Over the course of a week, the professor caught them ploughing a field that was too wet. He soon took over that. He found the couple stacking hay upside down, so that rain could spoil it, so he took over the hayfield. The young man's efforts to repair a fence by nailing the boards on the wrong side also needed the professor's experienced hand. By the end of two weeks, the professor had the farm up and running. On his last night, the wife cooked him a delicious dinner, because there was plenty of milk and lots of fresh eggs. He could hear the animals safely locked in their barns and pens, and all was in good repair.

As he left the next morning, he thought that the couple seemed a bit silent and depressed, but thought that was due to their having come to like his presence. He went back to his home, but intended to return the following year to see how the couple were getting on.

A year later he once again turned in at the farm gate. He was struck at how everything seemed neat and tidy. There was an air of prosperity to the place, and it made him smile in satisfaction. He knocked on the farmhouse door, and was surprised to see, not the couple, but a middle-aged man at the door.

"Where are the owners?" he asked.

"I'm the owner," said the man. "I bought this place from a young couple of city slickers nearly a year ago. Got a good price, too."

"But why…" began the professor. "What made them sell so soon?"

"They told me that someone had come along and showed them how difficult it is to be a farmer. They said they'd never learn, and that they'd better try something else."

The professor said, "But I left this farm in good order,

everything working as it should."

The farmer said nothing, but as the professor neared the gate, he called out, "How did you learn farming, mister?"

"By making mistakes," said the professor. "My own mistakes."

Neither of them smiled.

The Strongest Trap

There was once a clever hunter who knew how to catch a raccoon. It's very simple, really: all you have to do is let the racoon catch himself. So this is a story about a racoon who found himself in the strongest trap ever invented.

The hunter took a nice, juicy fish and put it in the hollow of a tree. A racoon came along and smelled the lovely aroma. Now a raccoon is very intelligent, but also very greedy. The opening to the hollow was large enough for his hand—raccoons have hands, you know, just like people. He reached inside and took hold of the fish, but when he tried to remove it, he found that the crack wasn't large enough to let his hand pass with the fish in it. He was stuck. He stood in front of the tree, unable to move.

A crow was watching all this from a branch. He fluttered down and said to the racoon, "I see that you are caught in the hunter's trap."

"Yes," said the racoon pitifully. "I cannot move, even though the hunter will soon come and catch me."

"It is the spirit of animals like us to be free," said the crow. "To run and fly unimpeded through the forest, to go where we will, like the wind."

"That is true," said the racoon. "I long for my freedom now that it has been denied me."

"Then why don't you release the fish and run away?" asked the crow. "There is so little time."

"Because it is also in my nature to love fish," said the racoon sadly. "My instinct will not let me let a plump, juicy fish get away. Try as I might, I cannot take my fingers off it."

The crow pondered for a moment, and then said, "The hunter will make your insides into a pie and your outsides into a hat. He will come along any minute now, and you'll wind up in the pot."

"What shall I do?" wailed the racoon.

"There is only one solution," said the crow, looking at the racoon's sharp teeth.

And that is why, in some parts of the world, they say so-and-so is as greedy as a three-legged racoon.

The Locksmith's Escape

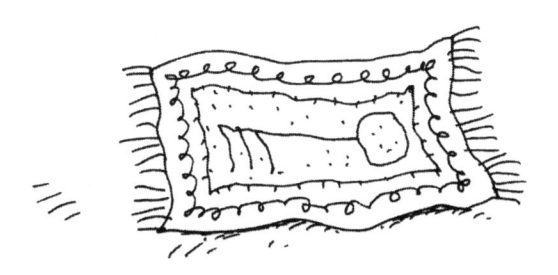

A disenchanted young man asked his mullah, "What good is prayer, anyway? I pray five times a day, just like everyone else, and things never seem to get any better or any worse." The mullah responded with this tale:

A certain locksmith of devout habits managed to get into a disagreement with the Emperor. He was convicted of a false crime on trumped-up charges and locked into a small cell, barely wider than his arms could reach.

His family wept, but the locksmith remained calm and said, "God will rescue me." The chief gaoler, sympathetic to the injustice but fearful to get into trouble with His Majesty, asked the prisoner if there was anything he could bring him to ease his time in confinement.

"Yes," said the locksmith. "I would like a prayer mat." After much discussion at his mosque, some friends commissioned a new mat from a master weaver. A rug with intricate patterns arrived shortly and the locksmith used it faithfully. Each day at the call of the muezzin which filtered through the high single window in his cell the locksmith bowed in prayer.

Time passed. Months became years. The old Emperor died, but no one in the new regime did anything to reduce his sentence. The locksmith's beard grew long and turned white, but he still appeared unruffled. "God will rescue me," is all he would say, and continued bowing his forehead to the ornate mat, five times every day.

His devotion became famous in the prison, and finally throughout the town. Guards treated him with respect, but still carefully locked the cell door each time they left. Ten years passed, then twenty.

One day the new chief gaoler, the son of the former official who had retired, stopped by the locksmith's cell, as was his habit, to greet the holy man. He was amazed to find that the cell door was standing open, and the locksmith gone.

"God must have rescued him at last," was all he said, scratching his head.

Many years later, when the locksmith was an old man, someone asked him how he had managed to escape.

"After twenty years of placing my face on the prayer mat, five times every day, I finally realised something," said the locksmith. "Woven into the design of the carpet was a blueprint of the lock on the cell door."

The Spiritual Aspirant

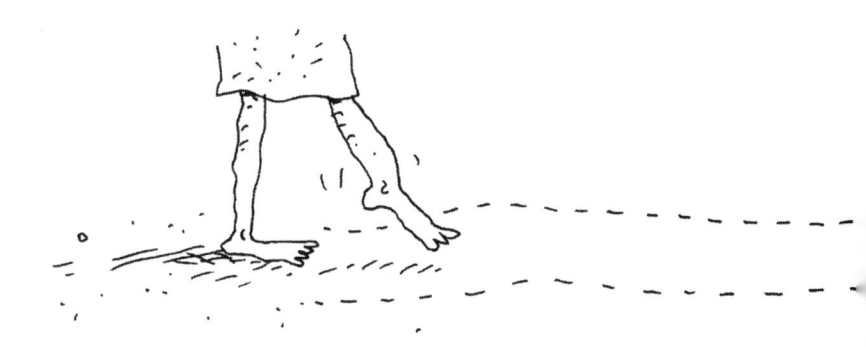

A seeker came to a monastery in a distressed condition. He had always wanted to be a spiritual aspirant, but he had lost any sense of the scriptures and of prayer. He went to see the head abbot, a wise man who was known for smiling continuously, even when things seemed difficult.

"I have lost my sense of meaning when I read the holy scriptures, Master," he said. "Yet my sole desire is to become a spiritual aspirant. What can I do?"

The master smiled even more broadly. "I suggest you spend one month here, reading the scriptures again and again until they mean something to you," he said.

The seeker stayed in his small room, except for meals. He slept only four hours each night. The light of his single candle could be seen through the high window. After a month had passed, he went back to the abbot, who asked him how he had got on.

"It is terrible, Master," said the seeker. "The more I read, the less sense the holy books make to me. As a spiritual aspirant, I should feel inspired. Instead, I feel completely lost."

"Hmm," said the abbot, still smiling. "Then I prescribe another month. This time you should spend it all in meditation until the sense of spirituality returns to you."

And so he did. He meditated through the nights, through thunderstorms and gales, ignoring everything else. After a month he returned to the abbot.

"I have failed completely as a spiritual aspirant," he said miserably. The abbot was smiling maddeningly.

"What do you want to do now?" he asked.

The seeker shrugged. "I suppose I shall return to the world and become an ordinary man. I cannot any longer call myself a spiritual aspirant."

The abbot's smile broadened until it became a hearty laugh. "Then you have succeeded at last!" he cried.

The seeker's jaw dropped. "But I am no longer a spiritual aspirant. How can that be a success?"

"You have put your foot on the first step of the path," said the abbot. "You now know that spirituality is a name without a reality. It will remain so until it becomes a reality without a name."

The Singing Creek

The professor turned off the winding mountain road by a large stone painted white, as he had been instructed. A rutted drive led to a house made of squared logs, half hidden by oak trees. A man in overalls of indeterminate age stood by the gate.

The professor rolled down the window of his 4x4. "Are you the Doctor of Happiness?" he asked.

There was no answer from the man except a possibly ironic smile. The man helped the professor park his car and lifted the rucksack from the driver's seat with surprising ease. The professor's room was a low-roofed addition to the cabin, and contained a wooden bed, a table and chair and a single window looking out onto a clearing in what now revealed itself to be dense forest.

"I want to make one thing clear before we begin," said the professor. He glanced frequently at a large wristwatch with a black dial and multiple hands. "I am here at the advice of my colleague. Actually, my… therapist. I have only one weekend for you to do whatever it is that you do." He paused, feeling nonplussed at his host's steady but friendly gaze.

"What is it that you hope to find?" asked the man at last.

"Whatever it is that I seem to lack," said the professor. "I am someone who has studied all his life. I am a scientist. I know how everything works. The facts of science hold no mysteries for me. But…"

"But?"

"But I can find no reason to be happy. Absolutely no reason to smile."

His host didn't speak for a moment. The professor counted the seconds. On the stroke of fifteen, the man said, "If all your study hasn't enlightened you, what can a simple old fellow like me possibly do?"

"My…colleague said that you could help people, and that that's how you got your name. Doctor of Happiness."

The man's smile became a chuckle. "What a wonderful title! But I am no doctor, you know. I have no degrees, no computers, no books. In fact, I can't think of a single thing that I could have that you don't have, and more."

"Well, there must be something," said the professor crossly.

"Unless your…colleague was referring to my singing creek," said his host. "That's the only thing I can think of."

"Singing creek? What on earth is that?" said the professor. "Look here, I didn't drive all the way up here for some sort of fantasy."

"No, I can see that," said the Doctor of Happiness.

A simple supper with scant conversation was followed by a night's sleep. The professor slept deeply and awoke to hear his host whistling in the other room. After breakfast, his host suddenly rose and said, "Now we'll see the singing creek."

A path led steeply down from the cabin through dense woods. Neither spoke. The professor was planning to make an excuse and leave as soon as this expedition was over. They came to a bank over a swiftly-flowing stream.

"Is this the…"

"Shhh," said the Doctor of Happiness. "Listen."

The only sound was of water coursing over rocks and past fallen logs.

"Do you hear it?" asked the Doctor of Happiness.

"Hear what? All I hear is the sound of water splashing over rocks."

The Doctor's face fell. "You don't hear the singing, then?"

"I hear, which is to say, a membrane in the aural canal detects certain oscillations in the ambient atmosphere brought about by certain predictable phenomena attributable to the science of hydraulics. That's all I hear."

"Maybe there's something wrong with the creek, then," said the Doctor of Happiness. He stepped nimbly into the stream and splashed across to where a log lay at angles to the current. He shifted the log so that it lay parallel to the stream. "There. Is that better? Can you hear the singing now?"

"What I hear is what any sane person would expect to hear. I hear the physical manifestations of the laws of physics. The alteration you just made, if any, is completely determined by basic principles of first-year engineering."

"There must still be something wrong with the creek. Help me," he said and began dragging stones from the bank and placing them upstream of the log. The professor sighed, but waded into the water and handed the Doctor of Happiness loose stones and bits of driftwood.

"Better now?" asked the Doctor, tilting a large stone on edge.

"First year engineering," said the professor. He dragged a large stump across the where the Doctor was creating a small island in the stream. The two men worked silently for several hours. Every few minutes the Doctor would put a finger to his lips and they would both listen for singing. The sun rose fully and both men removed their shirts. The Doctor pulled out a thermos jug and wrapped sandwiches from a shoulder bag. They sat in the dappled shade and ate in silence, while birds dipped and dived and butterflies hovered above the budding blossoms of hawthorn on the bank.

Toward late afternoon the Doctor heaved and rolled an oval rock from the bank and placed it downstream of his small island. The professor frowned. He rose and tipped the stone back toward the bank. "It was better before," he said. "You're ruining it."

As the shadows lengthened, both men sat on the bank in

silence. All thought of imminent escape had left the professor hours before. The Doctor started to speak. "Shhh," said the professor. He splashed across and opened a small channel in the island of stones and logs. The water flowed through in a small cataract onto a flat stone projecting from the surface. "That's better," he said.

In the morning the professor was not in his room. His bag was already packed and lay by the front door. The Doctor saw him emerging from the path just as he set the coffee pot on the stove. His guest was smiling as they exchanged greetings.

They ate in silence. Afterwards, the professor thanked the Doctor and announced that he was ready to depart.

"I see you are smiling," said the Doctor.

"Yes," said the professor. "I have been down at the creek."

"Do you still say that the sound it makes is just the-- what did you say?—'predictable phenomenon of elementary physics'?"

"Yes," said the professor, smile still in place.

"And that what you hear is just atmospheric oscillations on a membrane in the middle aural canal?"

"Yes, that too," said the professor. He rose, lifted his bag and turned toward the door. His back was turned, but the Doctor of Happiness could sense he was smiling.

"But now I can hear the singing."

The Secret of Happiness

The spiritual teacher was getting old and began to look for someone to replace him. There were two candidates: a young man who had excelled at meditation, at fasting and at singing. He was very popular among his peers, polite and well mannered. The second was a young man from a remote village who had always seemed shy and a bit backward in his exercises.

The master called them both and said, "I have decided to give you both a test, to see who is best suited to lead our cause in the future. I am going to tell you the secret of all happiness. But if you tell anyone else, happiness in this world will always be denied to you." He whispered in their ears, one at a time.

In the days that followed, the first young man went about smiling to himself. He said nothing to anyone. The second young man went directly to the marketplace and loudly told everyone there the secret of happiness.

The master called them both back and asked what they had learned. The first young man said, "I have learned that I can keep a secret." The second young man said, "I have learned that it is not right to keep such a secret, when so many people are unhappy."

Which was chosen to lead the monastery?

How to Make it Rain

It had been a long time since it had rained, and the farmers of the valley were getting worried. Row crops were stunted and beginning to wilt in the unrelenting heat and even the fruit trees were beginning to suffer. Up before the sun, everyone scanned weather reports and spent hours looking for clouds on the horizon.

The president of the farmers' association, who had a large acreage of peach trees, called together his neighbours one evening in the cattle market shed. He knew that if it didn't rain soon that he would suffer the loss of one year's crop, and if the drought went on all summer he would watch his mature trees dying in the field. Others who were in the same position stood silently. A few complained about the government, others blamed the Chinese for building power plants and one or two blamed the drought on the new preacher, whose fiery sermons pointed the finger at all of them and, besides, went on far too long.

A soybean farmer sighed, "Well, what can we do about it?

Nobody can make it rain."

"I can," came a voice from the back of the crowd. Everyone turned and saw a Native American wearing a bowler hat with an eagle feather stuck in the band. No one had noticed his arrival. Strange, because he looked outlandish in his soiled pin-striped suit over a sleeveless vest and a pair of worn-out cavalry boots with holes in the toe.

The president of the farmers waved him forward. "What do you mean? Are you saying you can make it rain?"

The Indian nodded. He was cleaning his teeth with a lock blade knife.

"My people were making it rain before yours got off the boat," he said.

There was an excited babble from the crowd. The leader shouted and they fell silent.

"How do you intend to make it rain, then?" he asked.

"That's for me to know," said the Indian, unsmiling. "But if you want water to fall on this dustbowl, I'm the man to do it."

The leader gestured for his friends to come forward. The Indian stood without expression, looking at the sky.

"OK, let's say we want you to try," said the head farmer. "What's it going to cost us?"

"Fifty dollars a head," said the Indian. "Cash."

There was more discussion. Some said the Indian was crazy, others that he was a trickster. A few said they thought they ought to give it a try. Finally, everyone reached into their wallets and gave the money to their leader.

"When are you going to do this...this magic?" he asked, attempting to sound shrewd.

"Right now," the Indian said. "Just as soon as the money is in my pocket."

Are you sure it's going to work," he asked.

"Always does," said the Indian. "Never has failed yet."

The stack of notes changed hands. It disappeared into the Indian's suit pocket without a word.

The next morning it did not rain. The farmers stood and looked into the sky for hours, but not a single cloud appeared. Row crops began to wither and fruit trees lost leaves. The following day was the same, and the day after. Two weeks passed, and the crops and trees finally reached a critical point.

"Where is that cheating redskin?" howled a few farmers from their truck outside the home of the head farmer. "If we we're going to lose our farms, at least we want our fifty dollars back!"

But no one knew where the Indian lived. People drove aimlessly about in the dust and rippling heat waves, but no sign was seen of the man who had taken their money. By sundown tempers had risen to boiling point. Everyone gathered in the cattle market. They had become a lynch mob without realising it.

Then over the roar of voices a noise could be heard. It sounded like drums coming from a distance, at first low in volume, but quickly rising to such a pitch that the voices of the farmers could not be heard over it. It took them some time to realise that it was the sound of rain, fat, heavy raindrops pouring onto the tin roof of the shed.

It rained so hard for three days that people could hardly leave their homes. They sat happily on porches watching the water restore life to the valley. When it stopped one morning, everything had turned green again and the sound of birdsong could be heard for the first time in many months. The president of the farmer's association drove his pickup truck out to the end of his fields to see what changes had occurred. On the dirt road, now pitted with mud holes, he saw a slight figure in a bowler hat walking slowly, picking his teeth with a knife. He was wearing a fancy new pair of western boots with an inlaid silver pattern. He pulled over beside the Indian.

"Some rainmaker," said the farmer. "I thought you said it always worked."

The first sign of a smile appeared on the Indian's face. "Oh, it always works, all right. Sometimes it just takes a little longer."

The Prophet's Rock

The story had been around longer than any of them. Fathers had told it to children and mothers had whispered it to new-born infants. Very long ago, the great prophet of their religion had stood on a high rock above the city, and with a final blessing, had ascended into heaven, leaving behind him a glow that overcame even the darkness of midwinter.

For many generations, people had made a pilgrimage up the stony path on the darkest day of the year to pray. Elderly and crippled people were carried in chairs by the strongest, and small children rode on their fathers' shoulders. At sundown, candles were lit and the singing began. It continued all the way back down the mountain path to their houses, where feasts were waiting.

Time passed, and the world became modern. Children grew up and went far away to schools and universities. But still the importance of this day drew them back to the high rock, which had now become the symbol of their faith.

One midwinter, two brothers returned from a distant city. One was a scientist, a geologist, and the other was a philosopher. They gathered in a party at their parents' house before the pilgrimage began. The geologist was looking subdued. His father asked what was troubling him. At first he just shrugged, but, finally, in a gust of emotion, blurted out his secret.

"Father, I am so sad to have to reveal something I have learned in my studies. But what is true is true, and cannot be withheld. The high rock of the Prophet cannot have existed in the days of his life. It is the product of an earthquake that occurred much more recently. So whether or not the holy story took place, it cannot have happened on that rock."

There was a stunned silence. Then people began to mutter things like, "But I have felt the presence of the Holy there…" Then the other son, the philosopher, spoke.

"But the Holy is there," he said. "Even if that is the wrong place, and even if—dare I say it—the events never took place, the Rock is holy now. It is we who make things holy through our devotion, and its power is undiminished by mere facts."

Truth, One Penny

A travelling monk, who had spent many years in search of truth, arrived in a village thirsty and tired. Remembering he had a friend, a fellow monk, who used to live nearby, he decided to try to find him. But the streets were long and crowded and he didn't know where to look. Deciding to go on, he started back the way he had entered, when he spotted a bearded old man sitting cross-legged beside the road. He had a small white flag on which were printed the words: "Truth, 1 Penny."

Intrigued, the monk approached. "You sell truth?" he asked jokingly.

The man did not smile. "Yes," he replied.

"I have spent many years wandering the earth in search of truth. And you say you can just sell it to me, just like that?"

"Yes," said the man.

"But how can you know the truth?"

"I know," said the man. His eyes were clouded and the

monk wondered if he was blind. He found a penny in his bag and handed it to the old man. "Go on, then," he said. "Tell me the truth."

"Ask me a question," said the old man, pocketing the penny. "Remember, you can ask only one."

"All right," said the monk. "Where is my friend, the monk Hui Seng?"

"Go back along this street to the second turning," said the old man. "Turn right and then enter an alley to your left. There are some stairs there. Climb them and knock and you will find Hui Seng."

Laughing and shaking his head, the monk turned back toward town. More in a spirit of amusement than inquiry he followed the old man's instructions. He knocked at the door at the top of the stairs. After a moment's wait, Hui Seng came to the door.

Amazed, the monk told his friend what had happened with the old man.

"But that's incredible!" said Hui Seng. "I have only just occupied these rooms today! How could this truth seller know that?"

After discussing it, the two decided to go back and ask the old man. They found him sitting in the same position, clouded eyes staring straight ahead.

"I will test this old man," said Hui Seng. "It is bound to be some trick. Truth cannot be bought and sold." He went over the old man and handed him a penny.

"Where can I find Hui Seng?" he asked.

The old man did not hesitate. "You have been looking for him for many years," he said. "I will tell you where to find him. But you may only ask one question. Are you sure that is all the truth you need?"

"That will do," said Hui Seng.

"Do you wonder why truth is for sale so cheaply?"

"It has crossed my mind," said Hui Seng sarcastically.

"Because the truth that most people seek is worth no more."

"Just tell me where I may find Hui Seng," he repeated harshly.

"I will do so. Go to the shop of the wealthy tailor in the town. Ask him if you can try on a coat. When you are wearing it, ask him if you can see it in a mirror."

"And then?" asked Hui Seng.

The old man looked up. His sight may have cleared for a moment, because he seemed to be looking into Hui Seng's mind.

"Then you will see Hui Seng," said the old man. "You could have had revealed the secrets of the universe. But now you have bought truth that is worth one penny."

X Marks the Spot

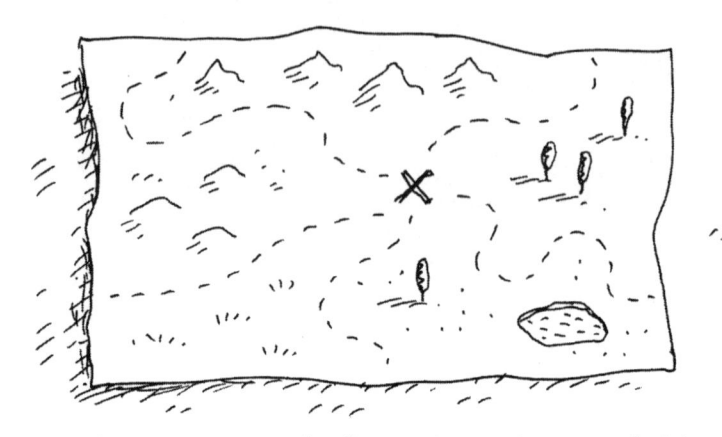

The father of a man who had adopted seven children had died peacefully in his bed. Being a man of great spiritual insight, he had agreed to care for orphans from a variety of religions. There were Muslims, Jews and Catholics among them—and even one Protestant. He had always made sure that each learned the practice of their own faith, so that weekends were busy with children attending mosque, synagogue and church.

But when the children grew up and reached adulthood, they began to quarrel. As they became integrated into their respective faiths they began to mistrust one another, so that by the time of their adopted father's death they were hardly speaking to each other.

A month later at the reading of the will, they gathered in an atmosphere of cold politeness. They learned that all of them had inherited equally. Each of them also received an envelope sealed with wax. These they opened when they were alone.

Each was delighted to read that they had been given a map that showed directions to a hidden treasure. But none of them knew that they had all received similar letters, and each one of them resolved to keep theirs secret.

The youngest daughter, who was a Catholic, could hardly wait. As soon as she had left her siblings, she tore open her envelope and found a map. In the centre was an X and the word "treasure". She was overjoyed, and thought how fitting it was that her father would have left the treasure to her and not to her brothers and sisters. After all, she was the youngest, and a girl at that. Her father, just as she had suspected, must favour the true faith.

The following morning she was up at first light. Leaving the village by back routes to avoid being seen by her family, she skirted the houses and made her way to a crossroad shown at the bottom of the map. A dotted line led her beside the river for a mile or two, then indicated a sharp left beside a large rock that resembled the head of a horse. She was amazed at how well drawn the clues were. She climbed a narrow track up a hill and then found herself at the edge of a large open field, where cows were grazing. Following the directions of the map, she climbed the fence exactly 50 paces along the west side and entered dense woods. Keeping the sun over her left shoulder, she went due west until, at last, she broke through into a small clearing, where a dead oak tree of enormous girth stood.

About to break into joyous laughter, she suddenly realised

she was not alone in the clearing. One of her brothers, a Muslim, was already there, leaning against the tree and panting from the effort of having climbed up a steep slope on the other side. His map, it seemed, had led him to the same destination, but by a different route.

"So," he said, it appears that Father has left his treasure to two of us!" The daughter tried to smile, but felt disappointment stealing over her like a cloud. Before she could answer, she heard thrashing on the left of the clearing, and was not surprised to see another of her brothers, a Protestant, burst into view. She could not help but notice the crestfallen look on his face when he saw the other two.

Before long, all seven children were sitting in the clearing. It became obvious that, though each of their maps contained different instructions, each route led them to the same destination. The eldest brother finally said, "Well, it seems that we are to share this treasure. What do you say we open it now?"

Each of their maps said that the treasure was in a small chest concealed under the huge roots of the old tree. They found it after a little digging and waited impatiently while the eldest brother opened the seal. Inside was a letter, nothing more. He read it aloud.

"Dear children, by now you have all assembled under this old tree, which I have known since the days of my childhood. In my memory it is still alive and covered with green, just as in your minds you may be able to imagine me, alive and smiling at you." The brother stopped for a moment and cleared his throat.

"The treasure I have to offer you is this. Always remember that even though all our paths are different, they all lead finally to the same destination. Look around at each other, sitting all together as a family. This is the way God has made his world. There is no treasure more valuable. So cherish it more highly than if you had found a pot of gold. This is my parting gift to you all."

The brother's voice trailed off, and they sat silently for a moment, lost in their own thoughts. When they looked up they saw that they were all smiling.

The Voice of the Soul

Once upon a time, very far in the future, the Intergalactic Council for Science convened on the ancient and decaying planet Earth, rumoured to be the original home of humanity. The occasion was the re-writing of history from the point of view of the new, enlightened age. Especially important was the expunging from the records of all reference to the superstitious concept of the human soul.

Everyone was in agreement except one member, a psycho-historian from the Betelgeuse Alliance called Abbar, who argued that you never knew when you might need a concept, no matter how outdated, and no matter how much space it took up in your database. The other Council members reluctantly agreed to allow him one month to show cause why the soul should remain in the cosmic record. The meeting adjourned, but Abbar remained on the tired old planet for a while, to enjoy its primitive mountains and seas, all recently reclaimed from ecological ruin.

One day a fool happened by. They struck up a conversation, and Abbar, amused by the fool's rustic manner, explained the problem he had been presented by the Council.

"Why that's no problem at all," said the fool. "I can demonstrate the existence of the soul quite easily."

Abbar was intrigued, but sceptical, when the fool outlined a simple plan. It was something that Abbar could accomplish with his own limited research budget, and for the life of him, no matter how he squirmed and vacillated, he could see no reason not to proceed.

The Universe is a large sort of place. When a place is large enough, there is enough room for almost anything to happen. And not just happen once, but many times, in almost the same way. So Abbar set about finding worlds where things happened in similar, and then in identical ways. His computers smoked and hummed for two days, but at last he was able to find two worlds at opposite ends of the Universe that were-- to all practical purposes-- identical. From there it was a relatively simple matter to find two individuals that were exactly alike in every way, down to their fingerprints, their male pattern baldness and their favourite kind of pie.

These two were both named Yan. They had had identical life experiences, married identical women, and had identical families and identical jobs as microchip recyclers. Both had the same annoying habit of snoring loudly and even had the same hairy wart on their noses. They were sent for, and arrived on Earth in time for the next Council meeting.

Even to the intergalactic sophisticates on the Council it

was a strange sight indeed to see two identical men shuffling their feet in unison, speaking at the same time in the same way, and looking at each other in astonishment. Abbar waited for the brief time slot allotted him, and with the fool at his elbow, took the floor. He explained to the two Yans that he was conducting an experiment for the benefit of science, and told them that they would be sent home after a few minutes. Both Yans looked identically relieved.

The fool whispered in Abbar's ear. The Council looked on, neither bored nor interested. After a moment, Abbar said to the two subjects,

"I'm sorry to have to inform you gentlemen, but I am afraid we have jumbled your records. We no longer know which of you belongs on which planet."

There was a rumble of voices from the Council and a cry of consternation from the Yans.

"But of course it will not matter," Abbar went on. "Because both worlds are identical in every regard. Your lives and experiences are identical. No one would be able to tell the difference."

"But I would!" cried the Yans in unison, and identical tears sprouted from identical eyes.

Abbar knew he didn't any longer need to explain to the Council. Everyone present was aware that what they had just heard was the voice of the soul.

Why White Folks are White

Long before the era of civil rights legislation in America, my family's cleaning woman, Carrie, once answered my childish question about why she was darker-skinned than I was.

Carrie was a church-going woman. She hummed gospel hymns all day. She sat in the back seat when my father drove her to the bus in the evenings, and sat in the back of the bus all the way home. She smelled of starch and was always, it seemed, wreathed in steam from the iron she wielded, ten to four, Mondays, Wednesdays and Thursdays.

I wanted to know why she was brown. She told me this story:

In the beginning of the world, everybody was the same colour as she is. Brown, black and shades in between. But people started preferring the ones with lighter skin, so everyone asked God to change their colour. They prayed and prayed, made sacrifices and badgered him until finally God said, "Enough! I will put a huge lake in the centre of the world. Everyone who bathes in that water will turn white."

Everyone travelled to the lake, all the people on earth. And everyone did indeed become white after bathing in the water, the same colour as white people are today—actually a kind of pink. But there were so many of them that the water began to dry up, until finally, when Carrie's ancestors got there, there was only a thin film left. Just enough to go on the palms of the hands and the soles of the feet. That's why everyone has the same colour palms and soles of feet today.

"So you were too slow," I said to her. "Your grandparents, I mean."

Carrie hummed again for a minute.

"No," she said, "Yours were too greedy."

Where Money Grows on Trees

While his elder brother had gone away to a far-off city to earn money to send home, the second son lazed around the fields, unwilling to do even a single day's work.

His father despaired. He tried encouragement, bribes, ridicule, and threats to change his son's ways, but to no avail. He sighed and told people that the young man was so lazy that he would starve to death in front of a full larder, because he was too indolent to cook for himself.

A letter arrived from the elder brother in. He spoke in glowing terms of the opportunities available to a willing worker in the city. He ended with these lines: "Here the money simply grows on trees."

To the farmer's amazement, the second son announced that he would go to join his brother. He was packed for by the family, driven to the bus depot on his father's wagon and duly installed on a coach that, after a three-day journey, would arrive in the city. This arrangement suited the young man, because he had to do nothing for three days but doze in his seat and look out the window at the passing countryside.

The coach arrived in the city after dark. Clutching the address of his brother's lodgings, the second son set out on foot. Tiring after just a few streets, he sat to rest on a bench in a small park. He dozed a bit and looked out at the green square of grass, where, apart from a solitary dog-walker who soon left, there was no one to be seen.

Looking through heavy-lidded eyes, the second son watched as something odd began to happen. A few yards in front of him a tree began to grow visibly. It sent out branches and rose several feet as he watched. Then it began to put out fresh leaves, but instead of ordinary foliage, the tree was suddenly covered with twenty-pound notes.

An hour later he arrived at his new lodgings and was warmly greeted by his brother. The second son sank exhaustedly onto a couch that had been made into a bed for him.

"You were right, brother," he said. "Money does grow on trees here." He told the story of the tree that sprouted twenty-pound notes.

"That's wonderful!" exclaimed his brother. "But where is the money now?"

The younger brother shook his head with exasperation. "I didn't pick any," he said. "Surely you don't expect me to work on my first night in the city!"

What is Goodness?

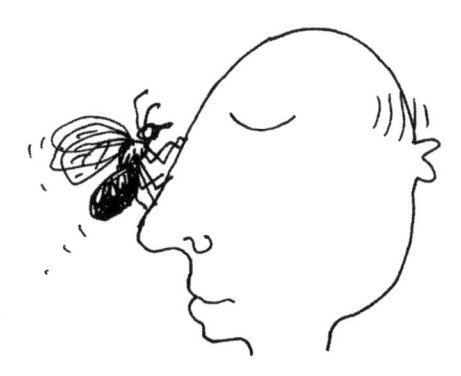

The pupil of the monastery was ahead of his peers in everything. He could meditate for many hours, so still that a fly walking on his nose didn't even cause a nostril to twitch. He could fast for days and still do his work in the gardens and his chanting was melodious to hear. Feeling that he had earned the right to be accepted as a full monk, he went to see the master.

"I have learned all that you can teach me," he said quietly. "I now wish to be an equal with you and the other teachers."

"Your progress has been excellent," said the master. "But there is yet one lesson you must complete."

"What could that be, Master?" he asked. "I have done all that this monastery can offer."

"Yes, you are right. Now you must go on a journey into the outside world and bring me back an answer to this question: 'What is goodness?'"

On his first day out, the pupil went into a nearby town. Seeing a ragged beggar holding out his hand for alms, he asked, "What is goodness?" But the beggar could not tell him, so he passed on.

Passing an overcrowded hospital, he saw a queue of sick patients waiting in the dust of the street. Approaching one old woman who was crying out for water, he asked her, "What it goodness?" But she could not tell him, so he passed on.

He came to a place where a small hut had burned to the ground. A man was crying out for aid, as the rains were coming and his family had no place to shelter. "What is goodness?" the pupil asked, but received no reply.

After several days of travelling, he returned to the monastery. He went directly to the master and told him what he had done.

"I asked many people the question, 'What is goodness'" he said. "But no one could tell me."

An expression of sorrow passed across the master's face.

"I didn't expect you to ask them," he said. "I had hoped you might show them."

The Most Spiritual Music

A famous spiritual authority, head of a seminary, invited four pupils to his home for one of his fabled dinners. Three were second sons from well-to-do families, who become priests as a matter of course. The fourth was a poor scholarship student from a peasant family who had struggled and then succeeded in being admitted.

There was conversation all afternoon, in which the head of the seminary listened to their ideas. Time wore on, but there was no sign of any food. The students were hungry, trying to mask the sounds of stomachs rumbling.

When dark fell, the master told them he wanted to identify the music that in their opinion most reveals the sublime. Three celebrated musicians came in and played first a reed clarinet, then a harp, and finally a flute. All this took time, and the students were growing hungrier and hungrier.

The master asked them to decide which music was more sublime. "First, who thought the clarinet was the most inspired?" One hand shot up. "The sound was like the sweet song of creation," said one of the wealthy pupils.

"The flute?" asked the master. Another hand. "It was like the breath of God," said another of the wealthy young men.

Finally the master asked about the harp. A third hand appeared. "It was like the very fingers of God as he created the world," said the third.

The fourth student did not respond. Just at that moment the servants entered. Food at last! As a great copper pot was placed on the table, a servant lifted the lid and tapped it on the rim to shake off the delicious-smelling drops of broth. At the sound of the clank, the fourth pupil's hand shot up.

The others all gaped, except the master, who said, "You are right, my son. To the hungry, the sound of a lid being lifted is sublime. And when you are as hungry for truth as for this stew, you will hear music everywhere."

The Meanest Man in the World

There was once a miser who was so stingy that he made it his life's mission never to give anything away. He had plenty of land and plenty of money, but despite the pleas of the poor and even his own family, he held tight to everything he owned.

One day he was crossing the river on a log. He could have used the perfectly good bridge that belonged to the miller, but that cost one penny. The log was slippery and too smooth to get a grip on. He fell in, in front of the whole village.

"Help!" he cried. "I can't swim!" he was floundering and splashing but his head began to go down.

Some people said they should just let him drown, because he was so mean. But most people were touched by his plight and decided to save him. They sent the strongest and most athletic young man out onto the log. He lay down and extended his arm to the miser, who was going down for the second time.

"Give me your hand!" shouted the youth.

Everyone could see the miser looking up at the young man. All he had to do was reach out to be saved. "Give him your hand!" everyone cried.

But the miser didn't reach out. He disappeared beneath the water for the third time, and everyone knew that he had drowned.

No one could understand why it had happened. They discussed the mystery for several days until a man said, "I know why he drowned."

"Why?" they asked him.

"Because the young man told him to give him his hand. If he had said 'Take my hand' the miser would have done so."

The Greatest Gardener

The Queen had reigned for many years. She was known throughout the land as a wise and gentle leader, and this made the people prosperous and happy. In addition, she was known as one of the greatest of gardeners, and could often be seen working alongside her grounds staff in the forecourt.

The palace was a site of pilgrimage for all of her subjects and many foreigners as well, because of the loveliness of the surroundings. A team of two hundred kept the shrubs and flowers, manicured trees and herbaceous borders, lilies and tulips and orchids in a perfect state. Even the bees were well organized and flew in orderly traffic patterns, and out of obedience to the Queen, never ever stung anybody. It was impossible to imagine a more perfect garden, and it filled the hearts of the people with pride.

There was only one part of the palace grounds which was not open to the grateful hordes. Behind the main palace buildings, there was a high wall enclosing a large space. This wall was so high and so strong that no one except the Queen could enter. Occasional children and other miscreants attempted to scale the wall, just to have a peek at what the Queen kept to herself, but the wall had been covered in glass and was too slippery to climb. No building in the kingdom was allowed to be built from which the garden could be overlooked. Even mad balloonists were prevented from flying too near the palace, and this was sternly enforced by a team of adolescents with catapults. The garden remained a mystery.

The head gardener had been for many years a dedicated servant of the Queen. When the time came for his retirement, he was sent for by Her Majesty, warmly thanked and given the kingdom's most coveted medal, asparagus spears rampant on a field of camomile. The Queen asked if there was anything she could do to make his retirement more comfortable.

The gardener hesitated, gulped, and then asked the favour he had been saving for this crucial moment,

"There is just one thing, Your Majesty," he said nervously. "I have been your head gardener for many years, but even I have never seen your private garden. We all know that Your Majesty is a superb gardener-- perhaps the most superb of all. I would call it a great honour to be shown your handiwork."

The Queen frowned, and the gardener could see that he had stretched his position to the limit.

"You may see my garden," said the Queen at last, "If you undertake to swear that you will never reveal the techniques that I employ in its cultivation."

"Of course, Your Majesty," said the gardener, exhaling at last. "I do so swear."

Without further ado, the Queen rose, and, ordering her attendants to remain in the reception chamber, led the gardener through a series of locked rooms and tunnels until at last they came to a metal door. The Queen drew a key on a golden chain from her throat, and unlocked the door. She turned to the gardener and said,

"You are the first to see this sight, you know. Perhaps you too can understand it."

The rush of sunlight dazzled the gardener as she opened the door. He rubbed his eyes free of spots and squinted. The garden appeared before him, a dazzle of green leaves. When his vision cleared fully, he beheld a weed-overrun patch of mere woodland. Wild vines tangled with un-pruned trees, nettles stood at head height, where unruly moths and butterflies swarmed. Rotting branches from dead trees lay on the ground, where muddy water had been allowed to collect. There was hardly a clear place to stand, but the Queen led him through a thicket into a clearing, where something wild and small scurried away into the undergrowth. There were rustlings and chirping from the trees overhead, where birds and lizards, snakes and -- who knew-- even bats might have their homes.

The gardener was stunned. He struggled to find words of comfort for the Queen, who was regarding him with an enigmatic gaze.

"I understand now," said the gardener, "Why Your Majesty guards this place so tightly." He cleared his throat. "But there is no reason to feel ashamed. Why, even the most demanding of your subjects would understand that a single woman-- even one as great as yourself-- could fail at cultivating such a raw patch."

The Queen smiled. "You think I am ashamed, then? That I have failed?"

"Regretfully, yes, Your Majesty."

"And you will keep your vow?"

"Assuredly."

"Then go and tell no one," she said, and showed him the door. When he was gone, she sighed deeply and sat on a bit of mouldy log. She was, as always, at peace in this place of wilderness on which all the order of the palace gardens depended, tended by the greatest gardener of all.

The Burning Question

A young seeker grew up with one burning question in his mind. While his friends all played games, he began to read books about God and religion. When his friends went to university and studied science and law, he took theology. When they married and had families, he kept on studying. He learned ancient Greek, Sanskrit and Hebrew. When they went on holidays with their families, he went to ashrams, learned meditation, fasted and chanted.

One day he saw his reflection in a mirror and saw grey hairs on his head. All those years of searching had not yielded an answer to his question, which still burned. Selling everything he owned, he went to live in a hut in the forest. In his life as a hermit, he continued to search.

He accommodated himself to his new life. He learned to live on very little. He made bread from acorns and stews from wild leaves and roots. He became so familiar to the forest that animals didn't fear him and birds would sit and sing on his shoulders. The years passed. One day, drawing water from a spring, he saw his reflection and realised that he had become a very old man. Just then he felt a hand on his shoulder. A voice said, "Don't turn around. You won't be able to see me anyway."

"Hello," said the seeker.

"I believe you have a certain burning question that you wish to ask me," said the Voice.

"But I have lost it!" the old man cried. "I have spent my life on this question and now it seems to have disappeared."

"That's because you have become the answer," the Voice replied.

Burning questions have a way of burning themselves out. When they do, nothing remains but answers.

Stop, Thief!

The teacher was always available to anyone who wanted advice on matters of the spiritual path. Many came to see him. They wanted all sorts of things: advice on investments, help with finding husbands for their daughters, and curing their rheumatic pains. But few visited him for guidance in truly spiritual matters. Or so it seemed, because the master knew well that the search for truth often comes disguised as something else.

One day a man knocked at his door. The master opened it to find a man holding a small boy by the scruff of his neck. The boy was struggling and trying to kick his captor. The master ushered them in. The man shoved the boy onto a stool and stood over him vigilantly.

"How may I help you?" asked the master, with a gentle smile.

"This is my son," said the man. "Or so I am told by his mother. I find it hard to credit, because since his birth he has misbehaved. I have tried beating him, locking him in his room, even starving him when all else had failed."

"He must be naughty indeed," said the master. He caught the eye of the boy, who was staring at him defiantly.

"Now he has been dismissed from school for stealing," said the father, in a desperate tone. "He has become a thief, and I am at wit's end. I cannot imagine that this wretched boy has any future at all."

"A future he undoubtedly has," said the master. "The question is what kind of future. Why don't you sit for a while, and I will tell you both a story."

He had not always been respected as he was now, the master explained. In his youth he had been wild and undisciplined. His father beat him and starved him, but the more punishment he received the worse he got. In time he grew to manhood, estranged from his family, and, inevitably, resorted to crime. He became a thief, who lived by his wits. He had never been caught. Because of his cleverness, he believed he never would.

The man gasped. "But you are renowned as a holy man!" he said. "How can one change so completely?"

It had happened one night many years ago, explained the master. He found himself with no money and no place to stay. Eavesdropping on conversations, he learned that a certain hermit, who lived in a hut on the edge of the forest, was thought to possess a fortune in gold coins. No one spoke to the hermit, nor understood his business, but the rumour had grown until the fact of his hidden wealth was accepted as fact.

Rubbing his hands, the young thief made his way to a stone hut on the edge of the forest. He hid himself and waited. He could see the light of an oil lamp through cracks in the door. When this was finally extinguished, he waited another hour to give the hermit time to fall asleep and then gently slipped the latch on the door.

The hermit slept silently. Treading carefully, the thief made a careful inspection of the hut. There was a table and stool, a shelf with a few simple foodstuffs, the hermit's wooden bed and a small wooden chest on the floor. Without hesitation he lifted the chest and slipped through the door. As he did, he heard the hermit stir. His voice called out, "Stop, thief!"

The thief ran away into the night. Carrying the chest slowed him down, but he was young and fast on his feet, so he quickly put distance between himself and the scene of the crime. Panting with effort, he stopped and leaned against a tree. He was astonished to hear footsteps in pursuit. A voice called out, "Stop, thief!"

The thief began to run again. However swiftly he ran, he could hear footsteps behind him, and the insistent voice calling for him to stop. He ran blindly through trees, tripping over rocks and scratching himself repeatedly with brambles. When he thought he had surely outdistanced his pursuer, he stopped to rest, but, each time, the footsteps grew near, and each time the same voice called out, "Stop, thief!"

As he ran, his fear increased. What kind of man was this hermit? Did he have supernatural powers that kept him on the heels of his intruder? Despite his fatigue, the thief marvelled. He must be some extraordinary kind of person to keep up this chase.

By dawn, the thief realised that he would not be allowed to escape. His crimes had at last led to his discovery. He knew that he would be caught, denounced and imprisoned, and that his life of freedom would be over. It was almost with relief that he stopped beside a stream, laid the chest on the ground, and turned to face his destiny.

The hermit came panting into view. He was a slight man, wearing only a robe of rough cloth. The thief could see that he too had fallen and been scratched by branches. As he approached, the thief noticed with surprise that he wore no expression of anger.

"Thank goodness I have finally caught you," gasped the hermit. "I was beginning to think you would run forever."

"I thought the same thing," said the thief. "But now I am caught. Do what you must."

"I ask you to open the chest, then," said the hermit.

The thief turned the simple latch and opened the chest. Inside there was a small stack of books. They seemed to be scriptural tomes, worn and obviously well-read.

"This is your treasure?" asked the thief incredulously. "And I ran through the night for nothing?"

"That is why I kept calling out to you," said the hermit.

"But these things have no value at all," the thief said. "You couldn't fetch more than a few pennies for these."

"You are right," said the hermit. "That is why I have brought you what you must have been searching for." He pulled a pouch from his waist. It was heavy, and the thief could see that it must be full of gold.

"Here," said the hermit, holding out the bulging pouch. "These things have no value to me at all."

"Did you run away with the gold?" The boy spoke for the first time. His eyes, like those of his father, were wide with wonder.

The master chuckled. "I helped the hermit carry the chest of books back to his hut. I lived there with him for seven years, until his death. He became my teacher, and that is how I come to be here now."

The man had put his hand on the boy's shoulder. There was now no trace of anger in his eyes.

"That is how I came to know that anyone can learn to recognise treasure if he persists." He smiled "Even a thief."

In Disguise

After God finished making his creation, as the Bible says, he saw that it was good. But something nagged at him. He called a conference of angels to ask their advice.

"I am pleased with the world, but I feel a little detached from it. I'd like to be able to observe it closely, not from this remote vantage point. Any suggestions?"

One archangel, a guy with a trumpet, said, "How about hiding behind a star?"

"No—you know how clever they are. One day they will invent space travel."

Another angel, a guy with a harp, piped up, "How about the bottom of the sea?"

"Same problem. They'll soon be diving down there too," God replied.

The room fell silent. Then a young angel, a guy with a bow and arrow, said, "How about a disguise? Make yourself seem ordinary. That way you could travel among them and no one would know."

"Excellent idea!" God said. "That's what I'll do."

"Which one will you be?" asked the angel. "Just for future reference."

"I'll never tell," God said.

Commandment number 11: better pay attention.

All the Names of God

A renowned holy man was invited to speak in a seminar at a spiritual academy. He came in after the programme had already begun and sat quietly at the back. The principal, a well-educated man in academic robes, seemed to look disapprovingly at the sage, who was wearing clean but rough garments. He was speaking about the spiritual path and how, as someone gradually learned all the names of God, he or she would progress along the path.

"„,and Allah, Ahuramazda, Yezdan, Ezad…" he said, impressing everyone with his spiritual knowledge. "And, of course, Brahma, Yahweh…"

When it was the holy man's turn to speak, the principal said, "Perhaps your holiness can give us more of the names of God, since you are renowned as a saint."

"Let's have tea first," said the sage. The principal grumbled, but tea was ordered and brought into the room by a servant, an old woman who struggled with the tray and cups. The principal spoke sharply to her as she slopped tea out of a cup. When she got to the sage, he spoke quietly to her. Smiling, she left the room.

When the tea was finished, the holy man stood up and said, "You are all hoping to learn the many names of God, am I correct?"

"Yes," said the principal. "God has many names and as an aspirant progresses, he gradually learns them all."

"Tell me," said the holy man. "What is the name of the serving woman who was just here?"

"How should I know?" asked the startled principal. "I am head of the academy and she is just a servant."

The holy man smiled and asked the assembled students the same question. They returned blank stares, except for one young woman in the back of the hall.

"Excuse me, sir," she said. "I believe her name is Anna."

"You're right," said the holy man. Turning to the principal, he said, "You see, God has more names than you think."

God in a Box

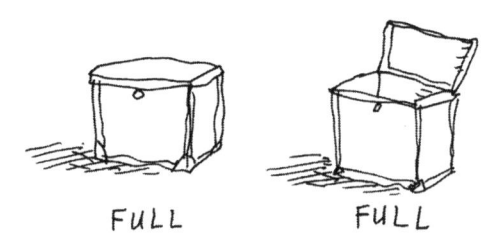

FULL   FULL

The little box sat on the table of the antiques dealer. Three men looked at it. The first said, "This box has an unusual history. It has been passed down for ages within a certain family, the last member of which has now died. That is how I came to possess it."

"What does the box contain?" asked one of his companions, a politician.

"It is said to contain God Himself," replied the merchant. As he saw the looks of astonishment on the faces of his companions, he explained.

The box had been the property of a certain demon, a friend of Lucifer. This demon used to get into debates with God soon after the creation of the world. When God remarked that there was no place he couldn't go, the demon dared him to go into this box. Then he closed the lid, and God has been there ever since, helpless to manage the affairs of the world. Which is why so many things seem to be going wrong.

"What do you intend to do with it?" asked one of his companions, a priest.

"I don't know," said the merchant. I have invited you here to help me decide. You two represent the State and the

Church. I represent the market. Between us, we should be able to decide.

The politician looked nervous. "In my necessary dealings with the business of the State, I have had to make certain decisions that God might feel were not right. He might even feel they were sinful, because He has been absent so long. I think the box should remain unopened."

The priest looked downright frightened. "My faith has not always been strong. I am afraid that I might discover that God is not as I have thought. I prefer Him to be locked away in a box, so that I can continue in my career without fear of contradiction."

The merchant said, "One of you fears punishment. The other fears a revelation that will ruin his life. I too prefer the box unopened. I fear it will lose value if its contents are allowed to escape." He put the box on a shelf behind him. "Let it remain as it is, a mystery."

Unnoticed by them, the young granddaughter of the antiques dealer had been listening. Before they could stop her, she reached across and opened the box. The three men gasped. They looked at the open box in her hand, which appeared to be empty.

"Silly girl," said her grandfather.

"Silly you," she replied. "Silly all of you. Of course God was in the box, just as He has been around listening to your philosophy. That's because if He is anywhere at all, He is everywhere."

A Difficult Beggar

Ancient wisdom has it that God is always on earth, but that He will almost certainly be in disguise. So children are taught to be as kind as possible to everyone, in case one of them turns out to be God. Even dressing as a beggar might be a good disguise.

Which is why, when Ali reached his old age and knew that he could not live much longer, he decided to travel the kingdom and discover God's disguise for himself. He had been a successful householder and was widely respected by his neighbours. His wealth was the product of a lifetime of careful husbandry. Having prayed and calculated for years, he had decided that the most likely guise God would use would be that of a humble beggar. So he gave his house to his daughter and her family, keeping only a small room for himself, sold his lands and gave the money to his sons, and turned over his possessions to an orphanage. He kept only one sack of 100 coins, to give away as alms, because if he met God in the disguise of a beggar, he wanted to be able to offer an appropriate gift.

In the city in those days there were many beggars. Cruel landlords forced innocent people from their homes and the uncertainties of the market place caused the ruin of many worthy men. Those with infirmities and those with bad fortune had no choice but to depend upon the kindness of donors.

Ali walked through the streets. At every corner he was approached by men and women in rags. Some knelt humbly in the dust, others clustered around and begged piteously for money. Each time he met a beggar, Ali gave him a coin and asked him for his blessing. Dirty hands were laid upon his head, a few prayed loudly, and, once, an emaciated scabby man embraced him while he tried not to shudder at his touch.

By the end of the day, Ali felt discouraged. Try though he might, he simply couldn't imagine that God was one of the filthy beggars he had met. The store of coins was dwindling, and the sun was already setting. He was about to turn towards home when he saw a large man sitting cross-legged in a doorway. The man was dressed in rags and appeared not to have had a hot meal in many days.

"Here, brother," said Ali, holding out a coin.

The man looked up at him without speaking.

"I want you to bless me," said Ali.

There was more silence. Ali could feel the man's hot stare

on his forehead.

"I cannot use what is given in greed," said the beggar, and looked away.

Ali wandered away, shaking his head. Greed? Why, his generosity must by now be the talk of the town! What a noble thing for someone to do, he thought. This meant the man could not possibly be God, or He would have recognised Ali's virtue at once.

The streets were dark now and Ali began to hurry. He had to pass through a neighbourhood that was infamous for its thieves. As he rounded a corner into a particularly shabby street, hoping to use it as a shortcut, a large figure suddenly loomed menacingly in front of him. He could not see the man's face, but knew at once that it was the same beggar, now revealed as a brigand, who might take all his money and even kill him. Panic filled him. He reached into his sack and grabbed several coins and threw them into the street. "Don't harm me!" he cried, and began to run.

But he was old and speed was a thing of his youth. He heard heavy footsteps behind him, and then a strong hand on his shoulder. He turned, knowing that he had met his fate. A hoarse voice said, "I cannot take what is given in fear," and thrust the coins into his trembling hand. The figure disappeared, leaving Ali shaken and even more confused.

Ali walked on, trying not to hurry and so fall in the road. Ahead of him he saw the light from an open door with a small group of people huddled together. What appeared to be a small family stood holding the limp body of an old woman on a makeshift stretcher. A loud voice could be heard from within the building. Ali realised it was the workshop of the carpenter, who acted as the undertaker for the town.

"I told you," shouted the undertaker, "No money, no coffin. No coffin, no burial!"

"But we have no money," said a woman. "We are poor. We only want to give my mother a decent burial. Won't you help us?"

"If I helped you, I'd have to help every miserable family of paupers in this town," snarled the undertaker. "Go and sell something and pay me my honest price."

As Ali approached, he could hear the sobs of the woman and her children. A man stood beside her, head bowed. Ali recognised the beggar who would not accept his money. Seized with pity, Ali thought, "This family needs my money more than any beggar". He thrust his hand through the doorway, holding the purse with its remaining coins. The undertaker took it eagerly, but, before anyone could speak, Ali hurried away into the darkness.

As he made his way home, a by now familiar figure stepped out into the road, blocking his path.

A hoarse voice said, "When your greed attempted to buy my blessing, I spurned you. When your fear attempted to buy your safety, I rejected you again. But I can always accept what is given in love."

"Who are you?" Ali asked, trembling.

He thought he could see a smile on the beggar's face, even in the dark.

"Now you have my blessing," he said.

Farming Wild Boars

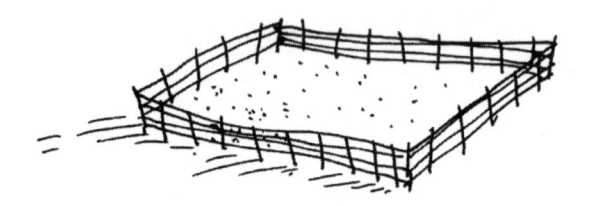

The meat of the wild boar is loved for its flavour and leanness, but it's very expensive to buy because wild boars simply cannot be domesticated. They are difficult to catch alive and able to break down the strongest fences.

A certain farmer always had plenty of wild boar meat to offer at market, and no one could understand how it was possible. A young and ambitious farmer wished to learn how this was done. He asked the farmer one day at market.

"I don't catch the wild pigs. They catch themselves," was the laconic response.

The young man decided to find out, so he hid himself in the trees and watched the farmer as he went about his chores.

On the first day he saw the farmer throwing corn onto the ground in the middle of a field. Then the farmer went away. After some time, wild boars emerged from the forest and ate the corn. When it was all gone they went away. The next day the farmer did the same thing, and the same thing happened. This went on for days, then weeks, until the young farmer was beginning to lose patience. He decided to watch for one more day.

The next day the farmer came out, threw the corn, and then quickly built a sturdy fence around the place. Then he went away. After some time the wild pigs came out of the forest. Finding the corn enclosed, they bashed against the fence until they had opened a space to squeeze through. Then they ate the corn.

Over a few days' time they had knocked down the fence so often that the farmer didn't bother to repair it. He just threw the corn directly into the pen. The wild pigs didn't bother to leave. Instead they just waited for the corn, safely in the pen. When the pigs were all fat and used to the pen, it was simple for the farmer to load them up and take them to market.

It takes just as much of effort to break into one's prison as it takes to break out.

Heavenly Pie

Once in a poor village a bad harvest had left nearly everyone hungry. The only crop that was available was potatoes, of which there were plenty. So the people ate potatoes: baked, boiled, mashed, fried, poached, sautéed and fricasseed.

The young daughter of one poor farmer told her family one day that she was sick and tired of potatoes, and that if potatoes were the only available food, she would live on water and air. This alarmed her parents. What if she began to sicken? She might catch an illness and die during the winter. They consulted the neighbours, but got no good advice. They went to the priest, who just told them to pray for her. They went to the mayor, who said she was just being selfish and should be sent to bed without any supper.

At last they heard of a wise man who lived on a mountain at the end of the river. The father made a trek to his little house to seek his advice. When he explained his problem, the man said, "Why not make her a nice heavenly pie?"

"What is heavenly pie?" asked the worried parent.

"I'll come along to your house and show you how to make it," said the wise man. "But first I have to gather some ingredients for my special heavenly sauce."

The next day he arrived in mid-afternoon. The family had eaten a meal of hash browns, but the daughter had sat stoically by. The wise man greeted everyone heartily.

"Have you got your special heavenly sauce?" asked the mother, wringing her hands.

"Indeed I have," said the wise man. "Now everyone go away and let me make my delicious heavenly pie."

The family sat outside. In the kitchen they could hear the wise man whistling cheerfully as he worked.

"Is it ready yet?" asked the little girl, rubbing her stomach.

"Not yet," said the wise man. "Making heavenly pie takes a lot of time."

Minutes passed, then hours. Smells began to issue through the window. Every few minutes the little girl would ask how much longer it would be. And each time, the wise man told her to be patient.

Finally, when it was past the supper hour and darkness had begun to fall, the wise man said, "I just need to add my special heavenly sauce to the pie and then we can all eat." Still more time passed. The whole family could hear the grumbling and growling of the little girl's stomach.

"Come and get it!" the wise man said at last, and the first one to the table was the little girl. She put her napkin under her chin and sat expectantly at the table.

"Now close your eyes," said the wise man. The whole family closed their eyes. They heard a heavy dish being set on the table.

"I'm just adding a little more of the sauce now," said the wise man.

After what seemed an eternity, he called out, "Now open your eyes and eat!"

In the middle of the table sat a dish of potatoes. There were mashed potatoes, boiled potatoes, sautéed potatoes and baked potatoes, garnished with chips.

"That's just potatoes!" cried the little girl. "Ordinary potatoes."

"It just looks like ordinary potatoes," said the wise man. "Heavenly pie sometimes looks like potatoes, sometimes like rice, and sometimes like corn bread. But what makes the difference is my special heavenly sauce. Now dig in."

The little girl put her fork into a pile of the potatoes and tasted them. Then she dug in hungrily, eating so fast that they could hardly scoop enough onto her plate.

"How was my heavenly pie?" asked the wise man, pushing his empty plate away.

"It was really good, "said the little girl. Sort of like plain potatoes, but not like potatoes."

"Ah, that's my special heavenly sauce you're tasting," said the wise man.

The little girl went off happily to her bed. The mother said, "Please make sure I know how to get that sauce, sir. I've never seen her eat like that before."

"You have plenty of the sauce already," said the wise man. "Its other name is hunger."

The Magic Lens

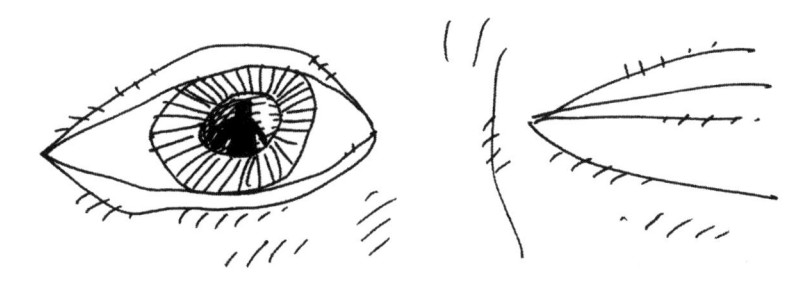

A certain old man was known to be very devout. He was not in good health, being lame in one leg and blind in one eye, over which he wore a stained cloth. He lived simply, played with village children and laughed a lot. When someone needed help with a task, or ran short of something to eat, he was always ready to help out. A rumour went about that he possessed a magical lens, with which he could see God.

A wealthy merchant of the town had spent many years trying to win the favour of God through giving money to charities and keeping the company of bishops and priests. He feared death and thought constantly about heaven. He was fair in his dealings, and always gave of his excess, but never of his capital. He felt that God would want him to be sensible, after all.

He heard the rumours about the devout man's magical lens. He thought, "Hmmm. With such a lens I could contact God directly, and that way win my way into heaven." He went to visit the devout man, who admitted him to his poor hut with obvious pleasure and served his visitor the last leaves of his tea.

"I understand you have a lens with which you can see God," said the merchant at last. He didn't believe in beating about the bush.

"I do, thank God," smiled the devout man.

"I would like to buy it from you," said the merchant. "I am willing to pay a very high price for it." The devout man smiled. "But that is impossible," he said, and turned the conversation gently away, toward the news of the town.

The merchant went away disappointed. He began to think constantly of the lens and how to get it. At last he realised that there was but one way: he would have to steal it. He thought: "After I have committed this small sin, I can contact God directly and be forgiven. There will be nothing between me and heaven then." He went looking in the market, and after some investigation, located a man who was thought to be the best thief in the kingdom. He employed the man with a few gold pieces and promised him a full sack of gold upon his delivery of the lens.

The thief agreed, and that night slipped into the house of the devout man. He searched through the man's poor possessions but found nothing. "Perhaps he sleeps with it under his pillow," he thought, and crept over to the man's bed. Gently, he slipped his hand under the pillow but found nothing. He was startled to see that the man was looking up at him, and even more startled to hear him say, "I am sorry that I have nothing to give you."

The thief fled in alarm. He went straight to the home of the merchant and told him what had happened. As he was talking, there was a knock at the door, and a servant admitted the devout man. He was carrying a small box in both hands, which he gave to the merchant. "This is all I have to offer you," he said.

The merchant opened the box and dug through a small heap of worthless possessions: a ruined penny, two little balls that the devout man used to play with children, and a torn and well-thumbed book of scripture. "There is no lens here!" he said in disappointment.

"No," said the devout man. The lens is here." He put a finger to his one good eye. "With it I saw God enter my home to steal from me, and I felt that I should reward his efforts, even with my poor possessions. "And with it I see you, who also are God, and I grieve in your disappointment."

The merchant sighed. "Then teach me how to use my two good eyes," he said.

The House of Spots

These spots have no meaning

Once upon a time in the unimaginably distant future, when people had survived a global catastrophe, and had been reduced to a state so primitive that no memory remained of past human accomplishments, a room was discovered inside a hill. Inside this room were stacked bundles of a substance never before seen. This substance was as light as a leaf and as clear as white stone and was pressed together into shapes that were straight and square, as nothing else in the world. The leaves were covered in even rows of spots of a dazzling variety and number.

The men who found this room guarded it night and day. The substance, it was discovered, made fires light quickly and burn brightly, and the leaves were useful in many remarkable ways, such as wrapping a parcel of berries, or for use instead of dry moss for personal sanitation. Over time, a small group was selected to guard the house of spots and to preserve it for future generations.

Some men, bored by endless guard duty, began to amuse themselves by counting the spots on individual leaves. They marked each spot off on one finger or toe until their digits were all used and then invented imaginary men to keep the count going. A contest developed, in which the winner would be the one who needed the most imaginary men to contain the numbers of spots. Soon afterwards, the multiplication of imaginary men became too tedious, and arithmetic was developed in the House of Spots.

Gradually, the guardians began to recognise and separate individual spots and learned to recreate them in the sand. These men became known as the spot-seers, or scientists. They acquired great status in the tribe. Ordinary people had never even seen the spots, but they held the spot-seers in high esteem. They provided for the living of the spot-seers. The best and brightest of their children were selected for training in the House of Spots.

After many years of arduous study, the total number of bundles and the leaves they contained was identified. A count was made of all the spots in the world. The mystery of the spots that had so baffled and awed their forebears was solved.

After several generations, a tradition of training young spot-seers began. In order to attain full status, a trainee would have to make an accurate count of a chosen bundle and arrive at the correct result. Each would also be required to accurately reproduce every known spot in front of a panel of spot-seers. In order to identify them, each spot was given a name. These were chosen by what the spot most closely resembled: a tree, a fish, a woman's breast. Some trainees became so adept at this that they could run down a row of spots and call out the names as they occurred, making a pleasant sound. Some of these sequences were memorised and became embedded in the tales told by night in the campfires and in the songs of children.

One trainee was practising chanting the names of the spots to his friends when an idea struck him. He shared it with his colleagues, who looked disturbed. Later, a venerable spot-seer called him to an interview. He asked the young trainee to repeat the idea he had shared with his friends.

"I think the spots are telling a story," the young man said, mustering up all his courage. "I think someone put them there to tell something, and I think each one of them has its own sound."

"That is a dangerous idea," said the spot-seer. "I will see that you receive punishment. You must never say it again."

The boy bowed his head, but as he turned to go, he said, "Why is the idea dangerous, Master?"

"The spots are spots and nothing more, and true knowledge lies in counting and arranging them. Any other idea is as much as to say that our mastery of the spots is not the pinnacle of human achievement, which it most certainly must be."

And that is why the spot-counters are revered even today, and why the notion of meaning hidden in details has no place in spot-seeing.

The Inescapable Cell

There was a certain burglar who was so skilful at breaking into places that, even when caught, he was unable to be confined in any cell. The king offered a reward to anyone who could build a cell so secure that the burglar could be trapped, and so give relief to his innocent victims. A man known as a fool announced that he was willing to build such a cell. Despite his misgivings, the king agreed to let him try.

He set about remodelling an ordinary cell and removed all the bars in the door except one, which remained in the centre. The burglar was brought into the cell, where he was cordially greeted by the fool. They talked in a friendly manner for a time, while the fool poured him numerous glasses of strong wine. The burglar bragged of his exploits, telling of times when he had scaled the highest of walls, slithered through the narrowest of cracks, hidden undetected in the palest of shadows. The fool showed his admiration and poured more wine.

At last he said, "Burglar, if you knew there was a jail that could contain you, would you change your ways?"

"Of course," answered the now drunken burglar. "I would

have to find new ways to use my talents. I would be forced to go straight."

The fool said, "This very cell is inescapable."

The burglar laughed. "I can escape from this puny cell in seconds," he bragged.

"Go ahead, then," said the fool.

The burglar got to his feet and swaggered to the door. There was only a single bar, but, because he was intoxicated, he saw double. He stepped between the two bars, but as he did, they closed rapidly and he struck his head and fell back. He shook himself and tried again, and again his head connected with the bar and fell back. He tried until his head was covered in knots. Then he sat beside the fool and wept.

"By some magic, you have built an inescapable cell," he said. And that very day he began taking correspondence courses, became a model citizen, and now always says "please" and "thank you."

The Light Bringer

Once upon a winter not all that long ago, the skies were unusually dark. There was a rain of ash from the sky, and many people thought that this might be the end of the world. Everyone was depressed, and they didn't feel like doing very much. They just sat around in their gloomy houses and sulked. The winter was turning out to be a drag.

The king was worried, too. If the people were depressed, they wouldn't work. If they wouldn't work, they couldn't pay taxes, and the king had his heart set on a new roof for the palace. He sent for his advisors from all over the country, who set about making spells and incantations, praying to every god the king had ever heard of, and a few that he hadn't. They even sent up balloons with gifts for whichever god was blocking the light from the world, but it didn't help; the balloons just popped and the gifts fell to earth, where greedy people helped themselves.

The king heard that a certain man known simply as the Fool was passing through town, and aware of rumours that this man was also wise, sent for him. He told the fool that he had little hope that anyone could help, but that he was desperate enough to try anything. The fool thought for a while, and then said, "If you will call a great meeting of everyone in the kingdom, I will arrange for the Light Bringer to be there."

"Oh boy," said the king, who didn't want to admit that he had never even heard of the Light Bringer. It doesn't do for a king to look foolish, however, and so he did as the fool asked. On the first day of the year everyone in the kingdom was invited to the largest hall in the palace.

On that day, the people sighed and crept through the gloomy streets, each one carrying a candle to at least shed some meagre light on their path. They began to crowd into the hall, and as they did, the room got brighter and brighter, and soon was lit up so well that the king had to put on a dusty old pair of sunglasses he had been saving for a sunny day. He peered out at the crowd.

"Goodness, Fool," he said. "It's so bright in here that I can hardly see anything except light. But where's this famous Light Bringer of yours?"

The fool looked out at the throng of people, who were laughing and basking in the brilliance they had missed for so long.

"Take your pick, King," he said.

The Man Who would be Rich

There was once a man who would be rich. He had tried unsuccessfully for many years to become wealthy, but finally had become desperate. Every venture he had undertaken seemed to lead him further into debt. Shops he had opened failed when a new road was built and diverted traffic away from his door. People began to laugh at him with each new idea. Try as he might, he could never seem to find himself in profit.

He read his horoscope in the newspaper, visited a palm reader and even slept with a horseshoe under his pillow, but all he got was a stiff neck. Finally, he could think of nothing but gaining riches, and as he did, his family and friends drifted away. He was reduced to sleeping rough, until he found a park bench that he began to call home.

One night he went to sleep and dreamt a dream. In this dream an angel appeared out of a cloud and hovered just above his park bench. He stirred uneasily in his sleep and opened his eyes to find that an angel was hovering over his head.

"I understand you want to become wealthy," said the angel, neither smiling nor scowling.

"That is my desire", said the man, stretching his weary muscles. It was still before dawn in the park, and there was no one else in sight. He rubbed his eyes to make sure he was not imagining all this, but the angel, dressed in white tie and tails, was still there.

"And yet you are sitting just a few yards from untold wealth," said the angel dryly.

"What wealth?" asked the man. He leapt to his feet so suddenly that he felt dizzy.

"You know that old man who comes here each day to feed the ducks by the pond?"

"Him? What has he got to do with wealth? Why, he wears clothing almost as threadbare as mine and just sits smiling at the ducks all day, feeding them stale bread."

The angel looked at his wristwatch. "He should be here any time now. He arrives early, just as the ducks wake up. Go and ask him to give you something and see what happens."

"But what would I say? I mean…"

"Trust me, I'm an angel," said the angel, and promptly disappeared.

The man who would be rich wandered in confusion toward the pond. Sure enough, the old man was standing greeting the ducks as they waddled out of the pond, carrying a large paper bag full of the day's rations.

Feeling foolish, he approached. "Good morning Old Timer," he said.

"A good morning to yourself" said the old man. He squinted. "Is there something I could help you with?"

"Well, er...yes," said the man. "I wonder if you could give me something."

"I don't have much of value, I'm afraid," said the old man. "But you are welcome to whatever you see that you like." He reached into his pocket and brought out its contents. There was a little change, an elderly person's bus pass, a half empty packet of chewing gum and a diamond the size of a pigeon's egg.

The man who would be rich felt his eyes bulge. Even in this dim light he could see that the gem sparkled with extraordinary brilliance, and that it had been faceted with great skill.

"What about this?" he asked, his voice trembling. He pointed to the stone.

"That?" The old man laughed. "Of course. It's of no use to me."

The man took the gem, fingers shaking. Trying not to look too hasty, he mumbled a thank you and tried not to run as he left the park. He stopped under the light from a coffee shop window and examined the stone. He was no expert, but he could see at once that the diamond was exactly what it seemed to be. Light danced from the facets like tiny sunbeams. It would be worth millions! He stood gazing at it until he heard footsteps behind him. It was the shop owner, coming out to raise the awning. The man put the diamond into his pocket and scurried away.

He walked until the sun came up, trying not to look like a man with a fortune in his pocket. This, he found, was not easy to do. People seemed to be staring at him suspiciously. It occurred to him that any jeweller he went to would do the same. How exactly would he explain how he came into such a possession? The obvious thing to think would be that he had stolen it. They might even refuse to give it back. Unconsciously, he turned up the collar of his stained jacket, even though the day was warm.

No, the first thing to do was hide the stone, so that he wouldn't be mugged or arrested in its possession. Perhaps under a tree in the park? No, that would never do; someone might find it by chance, or a magpie might carry it away. He shuddered at the thought. In a bank vault? But that wouldn't work, either. You had to have at least a permanent address to rent a safety deposit vault. Maybe he could just find a millionaire and sell it to him directly, taking a small loss, but solving his problem. That was it! He would find a millionaire and approach him. But where did millionaires go? He found he didn't even know.

After hours of walking the streets aimlessly, he found that, even though he was indeed the owner of a fortune, that he couldn't even afford a cup of coffee. Time after time he pulled the stone from his pocket and watched its dazzling surfaces reflect the sunlight. And each time his despair deepened.

By evening he was back in the park. The ducks, well satisfied, were gliding smoothly on the pond. The old man sat watching them, his face crinkled into a smile.

The man who would be rich found himself at the man's shoulder, and gave it a tap.

"Oh, hello," said the old man. "Have you been enjoying my little gift?"

"Not much," said the man. "I think I have come to trade it for something else that you have."

"Trade? But what do I have that you might want?" His smile seemed to deepen, and the man found himself looking into his peaceful eyes for the first time.

"I want whatever it is you have that made you able to give a diamond to a perfect stranger and then go on feeding the ducks," said the man who would be rich.

The Magic Ribbon

A weaver was passing through a poor village. On the outskirts of town he passed a small group of boys playing football in the dust with a homemade ball of animal skin and straw. One of the boys was sitting alone on the side looking downcast.

"What's the matter? Why aren't you playing?"

"They won't let me, because I'm too little."

"You'll grow up."

"Yes, but they'll grow up too, and I'll still be littler than them."

"Hmmmm. I think I have something that might help." He cut a piece of red ribbon from his cart and tied it around the boy's waist.

"Is that a magic belt?"

"Let's wait and see…"

On his return through the village a few days later, the weaver came upon the same group of boys. At first he couldn't see the boy who he had given the ribbon to. Then he spotted him in the midst of the game, playing happily. And what was amazing was that they seemed to be playing with a proper stitched football. After they had finished, the weaver called the lad over.

"What happened to your belt?"

"Oh, I was walking home and came upon the merchant. He had three chickens, but he couldn't carry them all. He could put two under his arms but the third would run away."

"So what did you do?"

"I gave him the ribbon so that he could tie the legs of the birds to each other, and that way he got them home. Sorry I lost the magic belt."

"But the merchant was very grateful, and look what he gave me!" he held up the football.

"It must have been magic after all," said the weaver.

What Noise?

I once lived in a village in Botswana, in a house that had a curse on it.

My wife and stepdaughter and I had all been pleased with the relative luxury of the cement block shack, because it had a tin roof and a high wall of shrubs all around. The place belonged to a Mma Tlokweng. When she came to collect the rent, she used to stand at the gate in order not to be affected by the curse. True, the outhouse had fist-sized spiders in it, and the solitary tree was inhabited by snakes, but we had no sense of bad luck until the first Saturday night.

In a shack some 200 metres distant, some off-duty soldiers from the army had acquired a grass-roofed rondavel to use as an informal night club. They had a generator and a set of speakers as high as a man and a clutch of electric guitars. That first Saturday, the gumba-gumba music began at seven o'clock. It went on until four a.m. the following Monday, with hardly a pause-- foreign, repetitive and off-key.

The glass rattled in the windows from the volume. My wife and I had to shout to hear each other speak. It was a palpable force that we could feel throbbing through the ground itself. By Sunday morning, after hardly sleeping at all, we were ready to leave, so we got into our jeep and drove to a shady place by the river and all went to sleep in the car.

I tried to remain cheerful. Surely it wouldn't continue for a second night, I reasoned. The soldiers probably had to report for duty bright and early on Monday morning. We went home at dark. The music was still in progress. If anything, it had increased. I had underestimated the stamina of young African men.

The music stopped abruptly just before dawn on Monday. I heard the dying rattle of the generator and relief washed over me. It must have been a special occasion, I told my exhausted family. A party, some celebration we knew not of. They didn't seem to believe me.

The week wore on, and I began to brace myself as Saturday approached. This time it began earlier, at about six. I looked at my despairing family and began to roll up bits of toilet paper to stuff in my ears. I found a few old cigarette ends, and discovered that the filters fitted nicely into place, but they didn't seem to help. More than a year later, when I was having my ears syringed, the doctor was astonished at what emerged. My wife wept silently, and my step-daughter seemed to be losing contact with reality. At one a.m. we got into the jeep and drove to the capital and checked into a tourist hotel we could ill afford.

That Monday, I sought advice from an old Africa hand I had met through mutual acquaintances. He listened sympathetically. "What did the chief have to say?" he asked finally.

"The chief?" I replied. I was vaguely aware that there was a traditional leader somewhere in the village, but had never even considered consulting him. "Can he do something?"

The old hand smiled "Try him and see. It can't do any harm."

The following day I stood in a queue of villagers in front of the chief's house, a traditional, mud-walled building, but larger and more sophisticated than most. I saw a new Land Rover parked behind it, and the rusty form of an air-conditioner jutted out of the wall. I carried, as everyone else did, gifts of tea, sugar and powdered milk. After an eternity, the people before me finished their tales of cow theft and wife-beating, and it was my turn.

Chief Solomon Dihutso greeted me warmly. I sat facing him on a stool so low that my face was at the level of his knees. He began by discussing English football, of which he was a fan. Then we turned to world politics before finally discussing the novels of EM Forster. By the time we got around to my complaint I had almost forgotten why I had come.

"So," he said, peering at me from a pair of filmy but possibly wise eyes, "I understand you don't like that soldier music."

"No chief," I said, aware of the understatement. "I don't like it at all."

"Hmmm," said Chief Solomon. "Would you like my advice?"

"Yes, Chief, please," I said, keeping my voice even so that I wouldn't cry.

The chief raised a single finger. "What I think you should do is…"

"Yes?" I nearly whined.

"Don't listen to it!" he said.

You Have Saved Yourself

A young prince from a noble family decided that, along with all his other excellent qualities, he should be recognised as a spiritual expert as well. He sought the approval of a certain spiritual master who lived in the forest. The forest was too dense to allow horses to pass, so the young man set off along a narrow trail. He arrived one afternoon, followed by a thin, sweating servant who was carrying all the equipment needed to maintain an important young man in comfort.

He introduced himself to the master, who sat in front of a humble hut, plaiting a rope from the fibres of jungle vines. The master nodded.

"And who is this?" he asked, indicating the servant.

"Who? Oh, he's just a servant," replied the prince.

The master smiled. "I see that you need saving," he said.

"Saving? Reverend sir, you are mistaken. I am a prince and possess all that other men would wish for: wealth, good looks, a promising future, and I have been thoroughly educated in all the holy texts. How could I need saving? No, I just want your recommendation of my qualities as a spiritual being as well."

"Very well," said the master. "I do detect a spark of wisdom in you, even though it may have been obscured by your upbringing. I will begin my work with you in just a moment. But first, take your servant and stand over there on that round wooden platform."

The prince looked puzzled, but obeyed. When he stood in the centre of the platform he scolded his servant to hurry over, carrying all his burden. The servant moved with trembling legs and started onto the platform. As he reached the centre, there was a sound of cracking wood and both men fell into the darkness.

They landed in the water of a deep well. The prince, skilled in sport, treaded water, but the servant began to flounder. His head would not reach above the water, and he was making gurgling sounds. The prince looked up and saw the face of the master, who had not changed his expression.

"Help!" The prince called up. "Save me!"

"I thought you said you didn't require saving," said the

master, "So you will have to save yourself."

"But the water is cold and deep. I cannot hold out for much longer."

"Look at your servant," said the master. The prince saw that the other man was nearing his last gasp. For a moment, he felt an odd sensation that he reckoned must be pity.

Just then, the master threw one end of the rope he had been plaiting into the well. The prince seized it and began to haul himself up until he heard what may have been the drowning gurgle of the servant. He looped the rope around the other man and tied it tight. "Pull," he said to the master. "Pull him out."

The struggling servant was hauled upward by the surprisingly strong arms of the master and lay gasping on the ground. The prince was at the limit of his endurance when he saw the rope again falling toward him. The loop he had tied for the servant was intact, so with his last strength, he placed it under his arms and allowed the master to haul him from the well.

When he recovered his breath, he said to the master. "You have saved me."

The master shook his head. "By saving your servant," he said, you have saved yourself."

The Master of the Rags

A young boy entered a monastery along with the others of his generation. Unlike them, however, he had been slow and backward at school and had left without knowing how to read and write.

The other boys mocked him, and he was at the point of leaving to become a wandering beggar like the other poor souls he had seen sleeping rough in doorways. One day the abbot found him sitting with head in hands, all alone while the other boys were practising their lessons. He asked the boy why he had not joined them.

Bursting into tears, the boy cried out, "Because I am stupid, Master! I cannot read or write and I don't understand the questions put to me in class."

The abbot looked at him for a minute than asked, "What can you do then?"

The boy thought and remembered how he had cleaned the windows of his relatives' houses and received high praise for it, the only praise of his life. Shyly, he told the abbot this.

"Then you shall become my window cleaner," said the abbot. "There are many panes of glass here that need a skilful hand."

So he did. On the first day he worked hard and all the windows, especially those in the abbot's chambers, were sparkling. But that was a very dusty country and overnight the windows became clouded again. On the second day he was lost in thought as he worked and did not hear the abbot approach behind him. He was startled to hear the master's voice.

"Where are you, my son?" asked the abbot.

"I was… I don't know."

"You must try to cultivate the quality of attention. From now on, when you are working, I want you to repeat these words, 'Clear the dust, wipe it clean.'"

From that day the boy repeated the words to himself constantly as he worked. He began to love the sound of them in his mind, as if they were a pretty song, and before long he began to speak them even when he was not working. He grew even better at his work, and because of the bundles of rags he carried with him he acquired a new nickname, "the monk of the rags."

One day he was cleaning the windows in the abbot's reception room and repeating his mantra to himself. The door opened suddenly and two finely dressed men came in, each followed by a servant. They sat in the two audience chairs and the servants stood humbly behind. The young monk made himself as unobtrusive as possible in a corner.

"Master," said one of them, "My cousin and I have come

to have you mediate in a dispute." The boy turned toward the abbot and found that he was no longer sitting in his chair. The second one spoke, and the boy realised to his horror that they were addressing him, thinking he must be the famous master. Tongue-tied and frightened, the boy stood mute.

"Not so much a dispute, really," said the other man. "But my rightful claim to some property which my cousin has seized without right."

"That's a lie!" shouted the first visitor and soon both men were shouting and hurling insults at the other. The monk of the rags stood still, unable to make a sound. When the shouting began to ease, one of the men looked at the boy and said, "You have heard our claims, O wise one. Which of us is entitled to the property?"

The boy was caught in a moment of terrible silence, with both visitors and their servants all looking at him. Where had the master gone?

The boy had never been able to answer questions in class, so how could he respond now? He gave the only answer that he knew, the one he had laboriously learned by heart.

"Clear the dust," he heard himself say. "Wipe it clean."

There was silence. All four visitors looked at him. Then to his amazement the two contenders fell into each other's arms, weeping.

"You are indeed great, O Master," one of them said while the other nodded through his tears. "We have been looking through the dust of self-interest, but now we see clearly that nothing should come between members of a family." Thanking his profusely, they left, arm in arm.

It was only then that the boy saw the abbot, peeping through the curtains at the back of the room. He seemed to be smiling.

From then on the monk was visited by many people seeking spiritual advice. He was known as the Master of the Rags.

Ripples

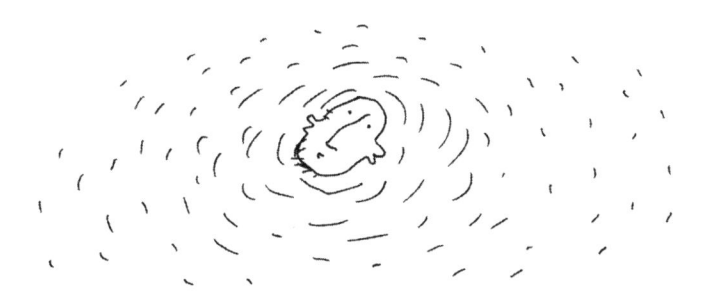

Two young monks were playing, when one of them insulted the other. The victim of the insult walked away scowling and the other watched him go. So did the master, who was sitting beside a small fish pond, watching the goldfish. He called the boy over and asked him what he had said to the boy who had left.

"I told him he was ugly," said the boy.

"Why?" asked the master.

"Because he annoyed me when we were playing ball."

"And where do you suppose he has gone now?" asked the teacher. The boy shrugged. "It doesn't matter," he said.

The master looked at him for a moment without speaking. Then he handed the boy a pebble. "Throw this stone into the pond," he said. The boy did.

"Now what do you see?" asked the master.

"I see ripples," said the boy.

"Now put your hand in the water and stop the ripples."

The boy obeyed, but quickly withdrew his hand. "I cannot stop them," he said. "My hands create even more ripples."

"Better to stop your hand from throwing a stone in the first place," said the master. "Now go and find your friend and see if you can stop those ripples."

99

The rich man was suffering from an unknown illness. He called for a certain healer, who was thought to be able to mend the problems of both the body and the soul. When the healer arrived, he found the rich man sitting at a table in front of a pile of account books. He had a twisted expression on his face and kept one hand on his belly, which was clearly in pain.

"I can't understand why I am feeling so poorly," said the rich man. "I have a lot of money, and with it I can afford the best food, the most comfortable home and employ the finest doctors in the city. But none of this seems to help." He indicated his belly and made a small groan as if by emphasis.

"Maybe the problem is not in your belly at all," said the healer. "And maybe the best food, the most comfortable home and the finest doctors cannot help you."

"Whatever can you mean?" asked the rich man.

"Come along and I'll show you," said the healer, and helping the ailing man, took him through a tangle of streets into one of the poorest neighbourhoods of the city. They stopped in front of a ramshackle house, where children wearing worn clothing were laughing and playing in the dust. A woman, obviously their mother, sat smiling on an upturned crate, knitting. A man was scratching in a small patch of soil where a few scraggly plants were growing.

"But these people are poor!" said the rich man. "What can I achieve here? I have spent my life avoiding such poverty, working day and night to acquire enough wealth to keep me from such a fate."

"Just watch," said the healer. They sat quietly as the children went on with their game and the man and his wife exchanged cheerful conversation.

"Why, they seem happy," said the rich man. "Don't they know how wretched their existence is?"

"No, they don't," said the healer. "What is more, they have the power to heal you."

"But how?"

The healer led the ailing man back home. When they arrived, he said, "Now I want you to call one of your servants and instruct him to carry a sack of coins to the poor family."

"What? Give away my money to such as them? How can that help?"

"Do you want to get well? Then do as I say. The sack of money must contain exactly 99 coins, not more, not less."

The rich man grumbled, but did as the healer asked. He realised that he was prepared to do almost anything to get well. The money was sent and the healer departed.

Days passed and the rich man's symptoms were not improved. With his servant to help him he went to the house of the poor family and spied on them through the gate. Things had changed. The children were not playing in the yard but carving clothes pegs from small sticks with knives. The woman was not smiling, but bent her back over a huge pile of washing that clearly belonged to other families. The man, with a look of fatigue on his face was stacking firewood that he had obviously brought on his shoulders from the forest.

The rich man was shocked. He had expected to find the little family in a joyous state after receiving a windfall like his 99 coins. And yet they seemed miserable, nearly as miserable as he. He returned to his house and once again called for the healer.

"So that is what the result of my gift is?" he asked sharply. "Instead of one person feeling better, now even more people are unhappy."

"And do you know why?" asked the healer. The rich man shook his head.

"When the money arrived, the family were overjoyed. But then they started to think, 'This money is almost 100. If we had 100 we would be wealthy. Let's hide the money away and work extra hours and scrape together the rest.' When they had accomplished that, they then said, 'If we can achieve this, then we can amass a fortune.' So they began to work even harder, stopped playing, neglected conversation and traded joy for industry."

"Those poor people!" said the rich man. He sat up in his chair and removed his hand from his belly. "It is the worry about money that has made them unhappy. And made me ill, too! From now on I will stop fretting and scraping coins and start living. I feel better already."

The healer smiled and said, "Wisdom comes in mysterious ways. Now you know what wealth is. It lies not in getting what you want, but in wanting what you get." He stood to leave. "Now you must excuse me," he said, "I have to stop by the poor people's house and see what I can do for them."

The Broken Jug

The master's little hermitage was high in the mountains, beside a stream. Pilgrims walked up the winding path daily to receive the great man's blessing. He was assisted by a young disciple, who looked after the old man's simple needs.

The blessing consisted of the master filling a beautifully decorated small pottery jug with water from the stream and then gently pouring it onto the outstretched hands of the supplicant, meanwhile saying a prayer. Many believed that he could heal illnesses and increase fortunes, but he just smiled and said, "The blessing of God is for all. I am just an instrument."

One day there were many people around. As the master was filling the jug from the stream, a small child rushed forward and collided with the old man. He dropped the jug, which smashed into pieces on the stones below. The crowd gasped, and the young man rushed forward. "Master," he said in anguish, "Does this mean the end of your blessings?" The old man just smiled and said, "It was just a vessel, not the blessing itself." From that day he dipped his hands into the stream and poured the water that way. And still the people came.

The following summer there was a terrible drought. Upstream of the master's hermitage a spring that had poured for longer than anyone could remember dried up. There was less and less water in the stream until one day it ran completely dry. The crowd muttered. There was a rumour that the master's power had dried up with the stream. But still a few people came, and the master blessed them with a simple prayer.

One morning the assistant went into the master's cell to wake him up and found him lying with hands folded on his chest. A smile was on his face, but it was evident that he was dead. The assistant announced this to the people who were already waiting for blessing, and they went sorrowfully away. After the funeral and cremation, the assistant returned to the hermitage and sat in meditation. He sat for a long time, thinking of the many wise things the master had told him. Finally he remembered the most important of all.

He let it be known that blessings were still conducted in the hermitage, and slowly, people began to return. When they came, he asked them to pray for one another. When asked about the loss of the master, he always said, "It was just the vessel, not the blessing itself."

Dinnertime in Heaven

A holy man had prayed without ceasing for many years. His knees had grown calluses from the time he spent on them, and his palms nearly grew together from being so often in contact. He prayed for many things, but what concerned him most was the afterlife.

All his days he had imagined a time when he would enter paradise, but, even though he was more devout than anyone else he knew, he also feared hell. His prayers focussed on knowing what these two places were like, to the exclusion of anything else.

The other brothers of the monastery wasted their time in doing work among the poor, running a clinic and feeding great numbers of unfortunates from a large cauldron of soup every evening. But the holy man was fixated on his goal.

So perhaps he should not have been surprised one evening when, in the fifth hour on his knees, an angel appeared in his cell. The angel was a magnificent being, neither male nor female, old not young, fierce nor especially friendly.

"You had a request, I believe?" said the angel.

The holy man trembled with fear, but was able to say, in a quavering voice, "I want to know what heaven and hell are like." He rose to his feet slowly. "Er, please."

The angel didn't speak, but the holy man felt himself lifted off his feet and borne with tremendous speed in a direction that was neither up nor down, forward nor back. He opened his eyes to find he was in a corridor that seemed to have no end. He was also amazed to discover that he had an enormous pair of white wings that seemed to grow out of his shoulders. He found that he could work the wings and even lift slightly off the floor. But he also noticed that, because of the wings, he could no longer bend his elbows. He spun to see the angel hovering behind him.

"Where are we?" he asked.

"Hell," said the angel, and pointed to door that had appeared in front of them. "Have a look."

The holy man went through the door to find hundreds of people just like himself, wearing huge white wings and hovering around a huge table. The table was laden with every kind of delicacy: truffles, delicate pastries, heavenly elixirs in sparkling crystal goblets and exotic fruits piled higher than he could see. The others were also looking with longing at the feast, he noticed, but they were all groaning as if in terrible anguish. He saw that, oddly, no one was eating the food or drinking the wine. It took him only seconds to realise why: because they could not bend their arms, they could not feed themselves. The sight of the repast was torturing them all.

"Enough," said the holy man. "Please take me away from here."

The angel smiled and said, "Now it's time to see heaven."

The holy man blinked, and when he opened his eyes he saw that they were in the same place. There was the same table groaning with good food, and the same people hovering with their enormous wings. But this time everyone was smiling and talking happily. The holy man blinked and saw what it was the angel had brought him to see.

After a second he found himself back in his cell. The angel was still hovering nearby.

"Did you notice the difference" asked the angel.

"Yes," said the holy man. "In heaven they were feeding each other."

The angel vanished. It was probably just as well, the holy man thought. It was almost time to join his brothers in feeding the poor. A little practice just might come in handy.

A Donkey for a Cat

A poor villager came into the town square one afternoon mounted on a fine donkey. People gaped, because the day before, this man owned no livestock at all. "Where did you get it?" everyone asked.

The peasant smiled. "I traded it for my cat," he said.

"Your cat?" said someone. "That mangy old one-eyed beast?"

"Yes," said the peasant. He told the story:

A man and his young son were travelling to the city and passed near the next village, up the road. He was leading a fine donkey. Someone called out, "Look at that fool! He's walking when he could be on his donkey!"

Embarrassed, the man mounted the donkey and walked on. Soon, someone else shouted out, "Shame on you, riding in comfort, when your poor little son is forced to walk!"

The man got down and put his son atop the donkey and walked on, red-faced. But soon someone else shouted at him, "Look at the lazy boy, making his own father walk while he rides!"

The man joined his son on the donkey, who was now staggering a bit under the extra weight. Another voice called out, "For shame! Look at the heartless man overworking the poor beast!"

The peasant who was the new owner then said, "When he passed my house, the two were carrying the donkey between them. So I offered to help. He traded the donkey for my cat, which is much easier to carry."

Giving up Gambling

A great sage was also famed as a psychologist. A woman whose son was a compulsive gambler sought his help, and after some discussion her wayward son agreed to visit the sage.

"I love to gamble," the young man said, "But it's bad for my health."

"How?" Asked the master.

"Every time I win, the other players throw me out of the window. I wind up with cuts and bruises and once I broke my arm."

Later that day the son arrived whistling at his mother's house. "The sage really helped me a lot. I've changed my ways."

"Oh, wonderful! So now you will give up gambling?"

"Give it up? No way! But from now on I'll only gamble on the ground floor."

The mother went directly to the sage's home. "I thought you were supposed to be wise!" she accused the master.

"It is wisdom to know when someone will not change, and do what you can to help anyway," the sage replied.

Krishna's Chess Game

In a kingdom called Ambalappuzha, in southern India, a king once ruled who was renowned for his skill at playing chess. There were many poor people in the kingdom, who had little land for growing their staple rice. Legend has it that Lord Krishna, hearing the cries of the poor, arrived in the court one day, disguised as a mendicant.

The king's prowess at chess was such that he could defeat anyone with whom he had ever played. So great was his confidence that he made a public vow that he would grant anyone who defeated him anything his vast wealth could provide. It had been a long while since anyone had dared to play him, so when he heard that a stranger, even a poor mendicant, was bold enough to play, he immediately ordered the court to be put in readiness.

When Krishna entered the court, the king immediately ordered him to state what price he would exact in the unlikely event that he should win.

"I am but a poor man, Majesty," said Krishna, and my needs are few. All I require is a few grains of rice."

"Rice?" said the king. "Why, my good man, you can have palaces, land or bags of gold." He laughed. "But you have made your request. How much rice do you require?"

Krishna pointed to the chessboard with its 64 squares. "I would ask your majesty to pay one grain of rice for the first square, two for the second, four for the third. And then to continue until the board is complete."

"Why that is nothing," grumbled the king. "It is so agreed."

The game went quickly, and within eight moves the king found himself in checkmate for the first time in his life. He was dumbfounded, but, shaking his head, he ordered the rice to be brought, grateful that Krishna had not asked for a greater prize.

A large bag was brought into the court, and a servant counted out the grains. One grain was placed in the first square, two in the second, four in the third. By the time the first row was complete, the rice grains would not fit into the squares. Midway through the second, the bag was exhausted. Couriers started to whisper among themselves; the king looked worried. More bags were brought. They were counted and piled on one side as the sum grew. Within minutes, the king realised that all the rice in his stores would not meet the victor's request.

"O Stranger, what shall I do?" he cried. "I am a man of honour, and must pay my wager. But it seems all the rice in the world will not fill the chessboard!"

"Indeed not," said Krishna. "The total is 461 billion tons,

enough to feed everyone in the world for 27 years. You do not have to pay the debt all at once. Instead, you may serve the rice dish known as paal-payasam to all the poor of your kingdom as long as they require it."

To this day, paal-payasam is served without charge to pilgrims in the temple of Ambalappuzha.

Heed your Dreams

Ben's parents had both died in the war, but had managed to smuggle their son out of the country before they were arrested, shipped to a different country and executed without trial. He had grown up among strangers and distant relatives. He had been well treated and even educated, but he had always felt that his roots had been cut off prematurely.

The only inheritance from his father had been a small stone hut in a remote mountain range. This was where his father had spent his free time as a young man, hiking, fishing in mountain streams and composing verses of poetry. Soon after the war ended, Ben set out to see this sole relic of his family. His purpose was simple: if the place had any market value, he would sell it and use the money to bring home the bodies of his family and have them buried properly in a local cemetery, something he could not afford.

Arriving in the nearest village to the property, he asked the locals how to reach the property. Most were unsure, but at last he found an elderly man who knew the place. He also remembered Ben's father. He described the route at length, and Ben was shocked to hear just how distant it actually was. After listening to details of river crossings and ascents and descents, he was discouraged.

"It is remote, then," he said.

The old man laughed. "It is as remote as anything could be," he said.

It took Ben a whole day to reach the hut from the nearest road. At last, as night was falling, he arrived at the hut, scratched and weary from his travel. The place looked more than abandoned. It almost seemed unwelcoming. He managed to lift the heavy bolt that held the sagging door in place by making a noose of his shoestrings. By the light of his torch he could see that no one had been here for many years, except bats and other small animals. Too tired to investigate further, he unrolled his sleeping bag and slept on the stone floor.

He dreamt that his father was sitting by the fire, writing in a small notebook. Ben called out to him, but his father just kept writing. Suddenly he was gone. The notebook lay on the floor, and when Ben read from it, it said only, "Heed your dreams."

By first light he examined his property. It was a single room with a door, a small window looking out at the valley below and a stone hearth, in which was an enormous green cast iron stove with brass feet. He swept the accumulated rubble away with a broom made of twigs and started a fire in the stove. After making tea and ravenously consuming half of his rations, he took stock.

Clearly the place had no commercial value. Not only was it nearly unreachable, but it was in bad repair. It also lacked plumbing and electricity. Even the new generations of affluent families who bought vacation cottages would shun this place. The only thing of interest was the metal stove. It was unusual in every detail. How his father had managed to transport it here was a mystery. But that, too, seemed an unlikely source of sale value. How would he get it down the mountain?. As he sat musing, his father's words came back from his sleep: "Heed your dreams."

He spent the day exploring the countryside. He could see why his father had loved the place. The mountain scenery was magnificent, and there was no sound to be heard except the calls of birds and the motion of the wind in the trees. He finished his small store of food in front of the stove that evening and slept deeply.

And dreamed. In his dream his father and mother were holding a small wooden box and laughing. Ben looked more closely and saw that it was filled with gold coins. Once again, they disappeared, and once again the notebook lay on the hearth. In it were written these words: "At the place where the bridge cuts the rock, the giant dwells. Fight him for what is rightfully yours."

Ben awoke abruptly just as dawn was breaking, the words dancing in his mind. Making his tea, he thought how absurd dreams could be. Why this was the twentieth century, not medieval times. There were no giants, and gold coins had disappeared a long time ago. He had no interest in dreams. He shut the house as well as he could and started the long trek down the mountain. But a single phrase echoed in his mind with every step: "Heed your dreams."

He checked into an inn in town. At dinner, he asked the innkeeper, feeling slightly embarrassed, "Is there a bridge nearby? A bridge that cuts through rock?"

"Well, there is the old valley footbridge, about five miles from here," the innkeeper said. "It does pass through a cleft in the rocks. But it is no longer used. It is now in private hands. It belongs to a family that many people around here think is very odd." He dropped his voice, "They have a strange son, a very tall, unsociable sort of fellow. He has a house at this side of the bridge, and will not allow anyone to pass without paying a toll."

"What sort of toll? Where does the bridge lead?"

"Just across the valley to the main road. There is a new one now, one that will carry cars, so no one passes by there anymore." He looked around cautiously. "Besides, they are afraid of the son."

Ben felt a mixture of fear and excitement. The details of the dream seemed incredibly to be close to the truth. But on the other hand, he was no fighting man, and the idea of struggling with an anti-social giant was unappealing. He slept uneasily, knowing that he would have to go to this place and discover for himself what the dream meant. If he had considered forgetting the matter altogether, a third dream woke him at first light. This time it was his father, calling to him down the mountain slope, "Heed your dreams!"

The five-mile trek to the bridge was easy compared to the way up to the hut. By mid-morning he could see a slender strand of logs and rope jutting outward over the steep cliff to the valley and the river below. At the road, a huge rock had been cut by ancient tools. The marks of the chisels could plainly be seen on the surface. Ben felt a chill. A sudden impulse to flee gripped him, and he turned away from the cleft, but at that instant a harsh voice called out, "What do you want?"

He turned back to see a man dressed in what appeared to be a cloth sack tied with rope over soiled and ragged leggings. The man was tall and wide. His hair was long and matted. His features were coarse and seemed to be flattened. An unlit cigarette dangled from the corner of his mouth, leaving a trail of tobacco juice down to his chin.

Without knowing what he was going to do, Ben called out, "I want what is mine!"

The giant appeared to smile. At least his broken and yellowed teeth showed across his wide features.

"I don't know what is yours, Stranger," said the giant. "But I will fight you and if you win, you can have whatever you wish."

Ben knew he could not hope to defeat the giant in any sort of fight. His legs trembled. He felt suddenly very small and weak. But he heard himself say, "I will fight you."

"Good!" shouted the giant, and with surprising agility was upon him. Ben felt himself being lifted into the air, caught a glimpse of blue sky and clouds, and then landed on his back with a thump that shook all his bones. The giant reached down, grabbed him by the coat and once more lifted him into the air, where he shook him like a puppy shakes a rag doll then flung him twenty feet into a thicket. Ben could not catch his breath. He shook his head and started to rise when he felt the massive weight of the giant on his midriff. The enormous head looked down at him, smiling hideously, and letting fall a thread of drool. He began to shake, and Ben realised that he was laughing.

"You're no better than a girl," cackled the giant. "I could defeat you with both hands bound!"

Ben croaked, "You have defeated me."

"I haven't had a fight in a long time," said the giant reflectively. He removed his weight from Ben and sat cross-legged, looking at him. "No one will dare fight me. But at least you were willing to try." He gave Ben's shoulder a thump, which Ben realised was a friendly gesture. He stood up and hauled Ben to his feet.

"What was it you wanted, anyway?" asked the giant.

"I don't know, said Ben. I'm obeying a message I heard in a dream."

"A dream!" roared the giant, doubling over with mirth. "Don't you know that dreams are worthless? They are just a bit of night-time indigestion."

"Maybe so," said Ben, dusting himself off. "But I had to try."

"I can understand that," said the giant. "Why a few years ago I had a very powerful dream, one that came each night for a month. I dreamt that I found a wooden box full of golden coins."

"Really?" relied Ben, feeling a rush of something like fear. "What happened?"

"Well, I'll tell you, Stranger, since you were at least man enough to fight me. I went looking for the gold, but found nothing." He narrowed his eyes, "Don't you tell anyone, do you hear? I don't mind being called ugly and cruel, but I don't want anyone to know I'm stupid."

"I promise," said Ben. "Where did you look for the gold?" he could hear his own heart beating in the silence.

"I never found the place, though I searched for several days," said the giant. After a while I realised that there are no huts with a huge green cast iron stove with brass feet in these mountains."

Seven Fish

A British estate agent was vacationing on an island that had not yet been overdeveloped with hotels and fast food outlets. Bored at first, he spent his days wandering along the shore, where fishermen still plied their traditional trade, hauling their small wooden boats out of the water with winches onto the unspoilt beach. He sat for hours watching as men sat talking and mending their nets, watched their wives bring them hot lunches in metal pails. The whole thing was so relaxing, he realised, so authentic. People would love to come here, if only they knew about it. He started to think about developing the island as a popular tourist destination.

One day he approached a fisherman who was just finishing his net repairs and was pushing his craft into the water. The man responded with friendliness to his greeting, and, sitting on the gunwales of his boat, settled down for a talk.

"If you don't mind my asking," said the estate agent, "How long do you usually stay out fishing?"

"Usually four hours or so," replied the fisherman. "When I have caught seven fish, I come back to shore."

"Seven fish. Is that enough?"

"Plenty. I sell six to the fishmonger and buy bread and oil, and take the largest one home for dinner. I eat and drink with my family and friends and then do the same the next day."

"But, if you were willing to stay out a bit longer, say, two or three hours more, you would catch a dozen fish."

"What would I do with a dozen?" asked the fisherman, a look of puzzlement on his face.

"Well, you could sell the extra ones and invest the profits. After a while, you could afford to buy another boat, hire someone to fish for you, and increase your earnings."

The fisherman remained silent, so the estate agent rushed on. "In a few years you'd have a small fleet of boats, and you could afford to open a warehouse and sell your fish to other islands, maybe even to the mainland."

"And then…" said the fisherman.

"Why then you would have so much money you wouldn't have to work anymore. Others could do that for you. Your time would be your own."

"And what would I do with it then?" The fisherman seemed to be about to chuckle, but the estate agent couldn't see why.

"Well, then you could…spend time with your family and friends. And…" His voice trailed off.

"And go fishing," the fisherman said, laughing.

The Castaway

A man was sailing the ocean single-handed when he encountered a violent storm and shipwrecked on a small desert island. Nothing of the boat survived except pieces of wreckage, from which he built himself a crude hut. He eked out an existence eating coconuts and small fish, but knew that if was not rescued soon, he would probably die.

He decided that his only hope was for rescue from the sea. So he began to pray. Every waking minute that wasn't needed for basic survival was devoted to prayer. He prayed night and day for several weeks, but nothing happened. He became annoyed. He decided that he would give God a deadline.

"If You don't rescue me within three days, I will never believe in You again," he said.

Two days passed with no change, and his spirits dropped to their lowest point so far. On the evening of the third day a sudden storm drove him in to his shelter. Within minutes a lightning bolt struck the roof and the hut burst into flames. The man ran out side and collapsed onto the sand.

He awoke later full of bitterness. Still face down on the beach, he muttered," "It wasn't enough not to rescue me, but You had to go and destroy what little I had." He gathered his strength together for a pitiful wail: "So now I'm an atheist!"

"That's interesting," said a voice from above. "I'm a Methodist myself."

The castaway opened his eyes to see a uniformed ship's office leaning over him. "Where did you come from?" he asked.

"I saw your signal fire," replied the seaman.

The Chipped Cup

There's a wealthy man who lives in a lovely big house, which is well visited by friends and a large family. The house is finely furnished and well-appointed. But, strangely, in the centre of the great mantelpiece sits an old chipped ceramic cup. When asked about it, he just smiles, but we have managed to discover his story.

As a young man, he wanted to impress his school friends. They all came from families that were much better off than his. He was ashamed of his trousers, which, anyone could plainly see, had been let down by his mother as he grew. He was ashamed of his shoes, which were scuffed and a bit too small. He was always careful not to let anyone see his family's house, which was small and in the wrong part of town. Sometimes he walked alone in the wealthy part of town, looking in the windows and feeling envy.

One day the boys at school decided to go to the river for a picnic on the following Saturday. They would swim and eat lunch together. The young man wanted to go very badly, but he was afraid that they would discover his lack of possessions and laugh at him. Passing by the windows of a wealthy family, he noticed a beautiful gold goblet sitting on a table beside an open window. He reached inside, grabbed the cup and ran away. He looked at it in the privacy of his room. It was finely crafted and inlaid with semi-precious stones. If he took such an object with him on the picnic, he thought, the other boys would assume he was from an important family.

But as the week went by, he began to feel bad. His family were not rich, true, but they were honourable. There had never been a thief in the family before. He was unable to sleep at night. When he removed the cup from its hiding place, he began to notice that the gold object was heavy. It seemed almost too heavy to lift.

By Thursday, he was unhappy. He was not sleeping well at night, and his school work suffered. He began to worry that the police might find him and denounce him, making everything much worse. His friends would realise that not only was he poor, but a thief as well. After school he went home, and carrying the cup under his shirt, went back to the house where he had stolen it. The window was open. He crept up and reached through the window to replace the cup.

Just then a strong hand gripped his wrist. He pulled and twisted, but he was held tight. Looking through the window, he saw that an old man had hold of him. But instead of scowling, the man was smiling. A strong arm encircled him and lifted his through the window. He stood helpless, with tears streaming down his cheeks.

"Ah, so it was you who stole my cup," the man said.

"I wanted to return it!" cried the boy. "Honestly!"

The old man looked at him for a moment, and said, "Would you like a glass of lemonade?"

Not knowing what to say, the boy nodded. The man led him into the kitchen and prepared the lemonade, while the boy stood shaking. What was he doing? Was it poison he was preparing?

"Now close your eyes," said the old man. The boy obeyed, giving in to his fate. "I want you to taste two glasses of the drink," he said, "And tell me which tastes better."

A cup was held to his lips. The drink, despite his fear, tasted delicious. Then another, and the taste was the same.

"Now you may open your eyes," the old man said. "Which tasted better?" The boy saw two cups on the table. One was the golden goblet and the other was a crude ceramic cup like those his family drank from.

"They tasted the same," said the boy.

"So the gold did not improve the flavour?" asked the old man. The boy shook his head. They sat at the table and finished the drinks. The old man drank from the chipped ceramic cup and the boy from the golden goblet. They talked, and the boy confessed his shame at his family's poverty and his embarrassment around the other boys.

"Which is worse," asked the old man, "Being poor, or being a thief?"

"Being a thief!" the boy sobbed. "That's why I returned

the cup."

"So you are not a thief," the old man said. "And, because you are not a thief, I am going to reward you. You may take one of the two cups home with you. It is yours, freely given. Which one do you want?"

That's why, when the boy grew into a man and prospered, he always kept a chipped, cracked cup on his mantelpiece and just smiles when asked why.

The Object of Worship

There was a couple who made each other very unhappy. The man was obsessed with finding the right object of worship, knowing that if he could only worship the right thing he would be liberated at the point of his death. He tried worshipping everything: the sun, the moon, the tree spirits— all to no avail. The woman felt ignored and undervalued by this activity and schemed to find a way to make her husband appreciate her more.

One day she hit upon an idea. Browsing in the market she found a small brass idol, a figure of some unknown God from mythology. She took it home and showed it to her husband, claiming that she had had a vision that the idol was a representation of the most powerful god in the heavens. Overjoyed, the man placed the idol on a little altar and began to bow down to it.

He placed gifts in front of the idol, nuts and sweet things, and was happy to find that they were all gone by morning, proof that he had pleased this deity. One day he arose early and saw a mouse, heavy with a meal of sacred offerings trying to run away. Being so fat with food he was easily captured. He started to kill the mouse, but his wife stopped him. "Don't you see that this mouse is more powerful than the idol?" she said.

So the man began to worship the mouse. He kept him tied by one foot on the altar and fed him with sweets and nuts. One day a stray cat came into the room and ate the mouse. At first the man was panicked. Then he realised that the cat was more powerful than the mouse and was therefore more worthy of worship. He tied and fed the cat and bowed down to it every day.

A dog who lived in the street rushed in one day, and before he could be stopped, attacked the cat. The man got to him in time, but realised: this dog is more powerful than the cat. He sent the feline away and installed the dog on the altar. The dog was more of a problem: he barked day and night, and neither the man nor his wife could get any sleep. One day, overcome with anger, the wife untied the dog, hit him three times with her broom and sent him yelping out the door. The man watched in astonishment. He realised that his wife was more powerful than the dog, the cat, the mouse or the brass idol: it was she who should be worshipped.

The man began to bow down to her whenever he saw her. He made her presents of good things to eat and to wear, and for a time she was happy. But the man refused to let her leave the room where the altar was. He shackled her ankle to the floor and kept her a prisoner of his devotion.

The wife now realised that her cunning plan had failed. She didn't want to be worshipped at all. So one day when her husband was out she mussed her hair, painted bruises on her face with makeup, tore her clothing and lay on the floor when she heard her husband enter.

"Who has done this to you, O Holy One?" cried her husband.

"God did it," sobbed the wife. "The one and only God."

From that day on, the man spent his days in devotion to the one God, and the wife got on with being an ordinary, happy person.

The Rooster Prince

Two priests were old friends from school days. They had separate parishes in different cities, so didn't see each other often. One priest heard that his old friend had built a huge congregation and that his flock was exceptionally spiritual and active in good works, while his was still small and struggling. He decided to go and visit his old friend.

When he arrived in the city he went to the church but couldn't find his friend. After looking for hours, he happened upon him in a tavern, drinking, singing and telling jokes with a group of tipsy men and women. After meeting up with his friend he told him that he considered his behaviour shocking and could not understand how the priest had managed to have such a successful and pious reputation.

"Have you ever heard about the prince who thought he was a rooster?" asked his friend. "No? Well, let me tell you the story."

"There was a handsome young prince, who lived in the palace with his loving parents. All went well until one summer, when the prince suddenly announced that he was a rooster. He took off all his clothing, crawled under the table, pecked at scraps as they fell, and crowed each day at sunrise. When he was asked what troubled him, he merely clucked and flapped his arms.

The royal parents were at wit's end. All the resources of the kingdom were turned to healing the young man. Doctors were summoned, and then psychiatrists, but to no avail. Gypsies offered magic potions, faith healers prayed over him, but still he flapped his arms and crowed.

The king heard that a certain holy man was passing through the kingdom and sent for him. When the man arrived, wearing ordinary clothes and looking for all the world like an ordinary citizen, the king had doubts. But, because this was an emergency, he asked the man if he could help. After explaining the problem, the holy man said, 'I will do what I can.'

To the amazement of everyone, he instantly shed his own clothes and crawled under the table with the stricken prince. He crowed and flapped his arms, and after a few minutes of pacing and posturing, the rooster prince accepted him as just another chicken.

Night fell and still the holy man stayed beneath the table. When corn was thrown onto the floor, he too pecked at it before perching in a corner and going to sleep. At dawn, they both crowed in chorus. The king and queen wrung their hands and doubted. It seemed they now had two human chickens to deal with.

That afternoon, the holy man said to the prince, 'What's your name?'

'Why, roosters can't speak!' exclaimed the prince.

'But you are speaking,' said the holy man.

'True,' said the prince slowly.

After another few hours, the holy man said, 'I could use a nice ham sandwich.'

'Roosters don't eat ham sandwiches!' said the prince. 'But... will you share it with me?' In a few minutes they were both eating ham sandwiches with gusto and talking in low tones of matters important to poultry.

A few minutes later, the holy man announced that he was feeling chilly and asked for his coat. The rooster prince started to comment, but held his tongue. Within a short time, both men were fully dressed. Announcing that he was feeling a bit cramped, he stood up and left the table. The rooster prince followed suit. When the king and queen returned to the room they were overjoyed.

'So you don't think you're a rooster anymore!' exclaimed his father.

'Of course I'm a rooster,' said his son. 'But I also know how to be a prince.'"

The priest who had been caught carousing winked at his old school friend. "That's why you find me here in the tavern," he said.

The Speech

Mullah Nasruddin, the Wise Fool of Sufi lore, had been invited to make an important speech on a major topic at a large gathering of worthies. He arrived late, but finally on the dais, he asked, without preamble, "Do you all know what I have come here to say?"

"No," came the response from the audience. Nasruddin looked offended and at once left the lectern and stalked out, muttering that he wasn't going to waste his time on a group that had no idea what he was talking about. The assembly was horrified. A delegation was sent to find Nasruddin before he could mount his donkey and ride away. They appealed to him to return.

After a long discussion, Nasruddin entered the pulpit. Scowling, he asked, "Do you now know what I have come here to say?"

"Yes!" shouted the gathering, almost in unison. Looking even angrier, Nasruddin again abandoned the stage and stalked out, shouting, "Why should I waste my time telling you something you already know?"

Once again the delegates from the audience stopped Nasruddin and begged him to return. Reluctantly, he let himself be led back to the lectern. "Now do you know what I have come here to say?" he asked.

Half the voices of the audience called out, "Yes," while the other half said, "No." They were desperate not to offend the speaker again. Nasruddin looked solemn and said quietly, "I think you should avoid all this bother of visiting speakers, you know. Why don't the ones who know what I have to say tell the ones who don't?"

The Writing Lesson

The master took his star pupil on a long walk in the forest. When the young man asked the master what the purpose of the trip was, the master replied, "This is a writing lesson."

After some time they came to a fast running river. The master walked to the edge and then slipped on a wet rock and fell in. "Help me!" he cried.

The young pupil, knowing that he couldn't swim very well, quickly found a fallen branch and thrust it into the rapids. The master took hold of it and pulled himself, gasping, onto the bank.

When he had recovered, he reached into his bag and extracted a hammer and chisel. Pointing to a large rock, he told the pupil, "Write the following words on that stone: 'I saved the life of my master today.' Then inscribe the date."

The boy did so. After a time they moved off, and, finding a log bridge, crossed the river in safety. They spent the day on the other bank in silence. Toward dusk they started back. When they again reached the river, the master said, "Here, stop being such a lazy boy! Take my bag and help this old man across."

Seeing the crestfallen features of his pupil, he asked what was the matter.

"You were so rude to me!" said the boy. "For no reason at all!"

"Take this stick," said the master, handing him a branch. "Write this in the sand: 'My master was rude to me today.' Then inscribe the date."

The boy did so. When he was finished, he asked, "But won't the water wash away the words from the sand?"

The master replied. "That is your lesson for today. There are some words to be carved in stone, but others should only be written in the sand."

Un-chopping a Walnut Tree

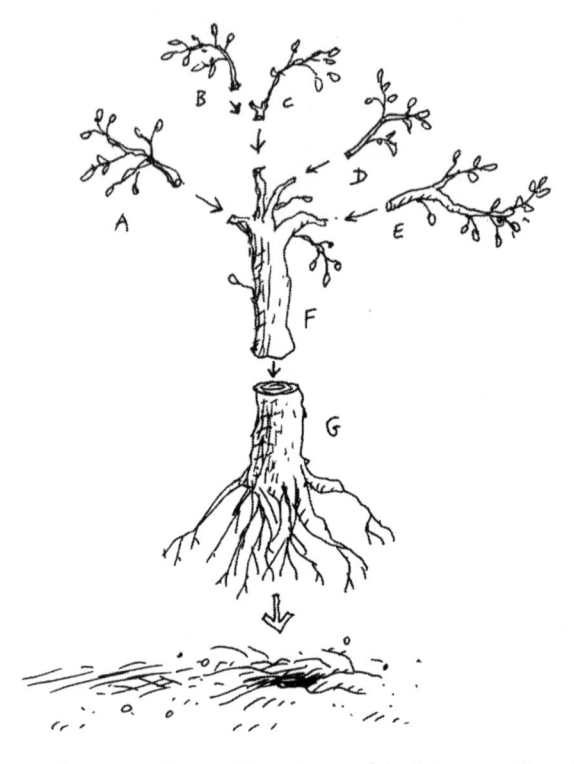

A man was clearing brambles from his big garden. The day was hot and sweat got into his eyes so that he couldn't see well. He swung his chainsaw and accidentally sawed through the trunk of a lovely walnut tree.

As you know, walnut trees take a long time to grow. It takes at least ten years to get the first few little walnuts and then many more to have a large shady tree. This tree had just given its first crop of nuts. The man felt so bad about having cut down the tree that he determined to un-chop it. From that time he devoted all his spare time to the project.

First he collected all the branches that had broken when the tree hit the ground. There were many of these, and he spent hours matching the splintered pieces and then carefully gluing them back into place. Then something awful happened: the leaves all began to turn brown and fall off. He carefully glued each one back in place and spent hours mixing paints to get the exactly right colour of green, then re-painted them. This part of the project took a long time.

He worked constantly. Sometimes he worked so hard that he forgot to go to work, and the bills began to pile up. Sometimes he worked so hard that he forgot to eat, and he grew thin. Sometimes he forgot to sleep, and he went around with both eyes half closed.

Re-attaching the trunk was very tricky. He had to pull the roots completely out of the ground to do this. He spent a very long time getting the rings to match exactly before he glued it in place. The next problem was the roots that had been torn out of the ground. He had to re-dig holes in the exact shape that would fit the roots. As the roots began to dry out, he rubbed expensive oils into the wood. Finally he stopped going to his job altogether, and just devoted himself to un-chopping the tree.

At last the tree was ready to be hoisted back into place. It was far too heavy for the man, who had grown weak through not eating and not sleeping. With the last of his savings he hired a crane and some men to help him. Over several days he rigged a harness that wouldn't hurt the tender bark of the tree and attached a strong chain to it.

The crane arrived and the man had to knock down a section of his fence so that the machine could get into his garden. He held the chain carefully up toward the arm of the crane, but one of the men said, ""Sorry, Guv—I can't get close enough." He pointed to where a young walnut tree had grown up during all the years of the man's labours. It was just at the point of bearing fruit.

"Don't worry," said the man. "I'll go and get my chainsaw."

The White Fat Little Dog

The kingdom was under attack by the forces of a neighbouring country, who wanted the land and wealth that was the envy of every ruler in the land. Everyone retired to the safety of the castle walls, but it soon became clear that the enemy was beginning a long siege.

Now a siege works by waiting until the people inside run out of food and have to surrender. At first this wasn't very worrying. There were stores of grain, cattle and sheep in the castle, and everyone was sure they could shelter inside and simply outwait the hostile forces. But weeks passed, then months. The people were dismayed to see from the castle battlements that the enemy had entrenched themselves for a very long wait.

As supplies finally began to run low, the king gave orders that, though he was sad to say it, all pets had to be abandoned and left outside the castle walls to fend for themselves. One morning the weeping citizens watched as their dog and cats were thrust through the portcullis and began sadly to wander away. All of the castle was now empty of pets.

Except for one.

This was a small white dog belonging to a little girl named Posey. Posey was considered the brightest child in the kingdom, always learning her lessons before everyone else. She could do her 11 times tables even faster than the teacher. She loved her little white dog, and after pleading with her parents, was allowed to conceal him under a barrel in the part of the courtyard where her family slept. All the family members gave the dog part of their own food. Posey had to sleep with him curled in her arms at night to make sure he never barked and gave the game away.

One day a nosey neighbour saw a small white tail wagging from beneath the barrel, and denounced Posey to the king's soldiers. The whole family was summoned to the court that very day. Her father stood in front, crumpling his hat in his hands in fear. Her mother wrung her hands and sobbed quietly. Posey, however, was defiant. She carried the dog in her arms, and when the king ordered his men to remove him, she grasped even tighter.

"Wait, your majesty!" she shouted. Everyone gasped. Children, especially children holding contraband pets, were never supposed to even address the king, let alone shout. "Do you see this little dog? Well, he can save your whole kingdom!"

"Whatever are you taking about, child?" asked His Majesty crossly.

"I will tell you privately," Posey said. "But no one else may hear."

Everyone gasped even more loudly. This child? A private audience with His Majesty? Unthinkable.

The king beckoned her with his finger. His scowl seemed to have been replaced by a look of startled admiration. Posey, without a second's hesitation, went up onto the dais and whispered something in the king's ear. Within seconds a smile spread across the king's face, erasing the care lines that had been etched there by the siege. He patted Posey on the head and cleared his throat.

"From this day forth," he declared in that tone only kings can muster, "This child and her dog are to live in the royal apartments. And…" there was a deep silence from the crowd. "The dog is to be fed first, the first mouth in this kingdom to receive even a morsel of food." He paused. "Well, that is, almost first. After Myself, of course."

And so it was. People watched in astonishment as the king went around the royal apartments whistling, accompanied by Posey and her fat white little dog. He was getting fat, as he ate and ate and ate, and his former trot became a sort of wheezing waddle. Soon he was almost too fat to walk at all. Meanwhile, people were looking thinner and thinner. The enemy troops showed no sign of being near departure. Everyone was looking worried. Everyone, that is, except His Majesty, Posey and the white fat little dog.

When the food was at the point of running out altogether, the king summoned a squad of his fittest-looking soldiers and gave them orders. Posey was looking worried for the first time as the men carried the fat little animal to the gates, opened them and let the dog go. The white fat little dog whined a bit, barked a bit, scratched himself behind one fat ear, and then waddled off toward the lines of enemy troops.

The enemy soldiers, bored with the siege, were happy when anything at all happened so they carried the dog to the tent of the hostile king.

"We found this animal, Your Majesty. He apparently escaped from the castle gates."

The king's face darkened. You don't get to be king, especially a hostile king, without being at least a little clever. The troops heard him sigh, long and loud.

"Tell the men to strike camp," he said. "If they have enough food inside the castle to let a little dog get this fat, we'd have to wait forever to starve them out!"

After the enemy left, the king handed back the fat white little dog to a relieved Posey.

"Bring this animal the last of our meat!" he roared. "He deserves to eat as he pleases!"

But Posey shook her head. "No, Sire," she said. "Thank you for the kind offer, but this dog is going on a diet."

Too Generous

A serving boy worked for a kindly master. He had no parents, but was happy in the rich man's home. One day the rich man died, and in his will left the boy a wonderful white horse, with a saddle ornamented with silver. He also left a letter, telling the boy that he was a kindly lad, but that he must beware of being too generous. On the day after the funeral, the boy set out to find a new life.

He rode all the first day, high on the beautiful horse, and came to a town. Everybody stared at him and his wonderful white horse. A crafty trader saw him and waved for him to stop. "Young man," he said, "you look like a kind lad. My home is far away across the mountain, and my poor wife and children are hungry. I have come to this town to sell my goat, which is an animal of wonderful value, for she gives ten barrels of milk a day. But no one can afford the price I must receive. It is late, and I am desperate, so I am willing to trade my marvellous goat for that horse of yours."

The boy thought: "I don't need so much milk. But this man needs my horse to get home, and I have nowhere to go in a hurry." So because he was generous, he traded the stranger his horse for the goat.

He continued on foot for the rest of the day. At dusk, he came to a farm, where a woman with ten children called out to him. "Stranger, can you help us?" she cried. "My children are all hungry and need milk!" She explained to him that they were so poor that they possessed only a single hen, who laid a single egg every day. That was not enough for such a big family. The boy felt very sorry for the little family, and thought: "If I give them my marvellous goat, they will have more than enough." So he traded the goat for the hen, and set off with it under his arm. He slept beside a field with the hen, and in the morning had a single egg for breakfast.

Later that morning he came upon a sad scene: A man and his wife standing beside a smouldering ruin that had been their home. Everything had burned, and the woman was crying. The boy looked with pity at the couple. If they had his hen, at least they would have something to eat, until they could start to rebuild their home. The man received the chicken in gratitude, and said, "But I have nothing to trade!" The boy said, "Never mind," and reached down and took a single nail from the ashes. "This is a very fine nail," he said. "I will accept this." And walked on.

As the day got longer, the boy began to worry. He had always been told that he must beware of being too generous, and now look what had happened! Instead of a fine white horse, he now had nothing to his name except a single nail. But he quickly forgot all his worries, because generous people live in a world that is generous to them.

At sundown he came upon a man in soldier's dress sitting on a rock beside a large black horse standing on three legs beside the road. The man was sad, and so the boy asked what was wrong. "I am a messenger, and I carry vital news of an attack on our kingdom to the king. But my horse has thrown a shoe, so I cannot ride like the wind to warn the king. Now the kingdom will be lost, and all because of something so small."

The boy exclaimed, "If only I hadn't given away my horse, you could have ridden him instead! Now all I have left is a single nail!" The soldier leapt for joy. "A nail? You say you have a nail? With that nail I can repair the shoe, ride the horse, warn the king and save the kingdom!" And that's what he did, riding like the wind to the palace. The king was warned, the war was won, and the kingdom saved. When the king heard what the boy had done, he made him a wealthy prince of the kingdom, and today he has lots of money to give away to people who need it.

People still say about him, "He's too generous!"

The Millionaire's Club

Verity had everything she wanted. She had her own room in a house with her mother and father. There was a garden in back with a swing made from an old tyre hung from a tall birch tree. She also had a cat named Puss, who slept curled up in her bed after her parents went to sleep. Verity had everything she wanted, except for one thing: a pony.

She had a picture book brought by Father Christmas which had colour photographs of ponies in places like India and America. Sometimes at night she would switch on a torch and look at the pictures under the covers and imagine that she had a pony of her very own.

A week or so before her birthday, Verity took a deep breath and asked her parents at the breakfast table if she could have a pony for her birthday. Her father looked at her over his newspaper. His eyebrows dropped. Her mother stopped washing dishes and looked at her father in that way grownups have when they are going to say something that children aren't going to like.

"A pony? Really, Verity. Where would we keep a pony?"

"In the garden, under the tree." Verity had been thinking it through.

"Do you have any idea how much a pony costs?" asked her mother. "How would we feed it?"

"Well, they eat grass, don't they? We have lots of grass, and then Daddy wouldn't have to mow the lawn."

There was a long silence. Finally her father said, with another look at the mother, "I'm afraid that's out of the question, dear. A person would have to be a millionaire these days to own a pony."

He went back to his newspaper, and Verity went to her room, where she could cry in peace. She thought about what her father had said all the way to school, and she thought about it all day. So much so that she could hardly pay attention to the lesson. Instead she drew pictures of ponies that no one saw.

That night she stayed in her room, even when her mother asked if she wanted a cup of hot chocolate. She kept the Pony book under her pillow, and after the lights were out, she stared at it for a long time.

A millionaire, her father had said. She wasn't even sure what a millionaire was, but she knew it must be something unusual. Her frustration grew, and finally she said to the cat, who was already asleep, "I wish I was a millionaire!"

There was a strange whooshing noise, like the sound of a

roman candle just before it explodes, from one corner of her room. She looked up to see a man leaning against the wall. He was short, with a stomach that fell over his trousers. He wore a brown suit and polka-dot tie and had a briefcase in his hand. He was bald except for a fringe of hair around his ears and a small chin beard. He didn't seem much taller than she was.

"Who are you?" she asked, wondering that she wasn't afraid.

"A genie," said the little man in a high-pitched voice. "At your service."

"Is that like a fairy?" asked Verity, who didn't know what a genie was, actually.

"Mind your tongue," snapped the genie. "Do I look like a fairy to you?"

"Well, I..."

"I am here to process your request," said the little man in a business-like way.

"What request?" asked Verity.

"Why, your application for membership in the Millionaire's Club, of course."

"But I..."

"Perfectly straight forward. I process your application, which should be accepted without any difficulty." He looked around her room with an expression of distaste. "I can see why you have applied for membership, I must say."

"But I'm not a millionaire," said Verity.

"Of course not," the genie snapped. He sighed, "If you

were a millionaire you would already be a member, now wouldn't you?"

Verity said nothing. She was beginning to feel excited. A millionaire! If she were a millionaire, she could have a pony of her own, and Dad couldn't say anything.

"Well?" the man said. "Are you coming?"

"Where?"

The genie seemed to be controlling his temper. Carefully he said, "To where millionaires live, of course. Honestly!" He spun his briefcase rapidly and Verity heard the whooshing sound again. She closed her eyes, and when she opened them again she found herself standing in front of an enormous house with high white columns and a fountain in the front garden. All around were high hedges, and over these, a view of mountains. The road she was standing on stretched away through some beautifully tended trees. She spun around in panic, but the genie was still there. His briefcase had stopped spinning.

"Where are we?" Verity asked.

"At your new home," said the genie. "Why don't you go inside?"

"As she approached the huge front door, it opened silently. Inside were two footmen, one on either side, who bowed when they saw her. She walked across a large shining floor that ended in a marble staircase that went up and up until it seemed to reach a skylight that looked like the windows in her church.

Verity ran upstairs. This was exciting! The walls were covered with paintings of men and women on horseback. One of them even had a picture of a pony.

"Whose is all this?" she asked excitedly to the genie, who was puffing up the staircase behind her.

"It's yours, naturally. Your millionaire's residence."

Hers! All of this! She ran from room to room, all of which had high ceilings, tall windows leading onto balconies and expensive-looking furniture. She laughed and ran out onto a balcony that overlooked acres and acres of land with green grass.

"Why, I could keep a pony here!" she said. "There's plenty of grass!"

"Look to your left," said the genie. "Over there."

She saw tiny white and brown dots that seemed no bigger than insects in the distance. "Those are your ponies," aid the genie. "I think there are a few dozen in that particular herd."

Verity felt alarmed. "Oh, but I just want one," she said. "One pony that I can look after."

The genie shook his head. "Oh no. You won't be looking after any ponies. You're a millionaire now. Millionaires don't look after their own livestock. You have grooms and stable masters to do that."

Verity didn't answer. Maybe after the genie was gone, she could just pick one of the ponies and look after him all she pleased.

"I think I'll take this bedroom," she said, opening a door.

In the middle of a floor big enough to roller skate on, there was a bed with four posts and a tent over. "Puss will like such a big bed!"

The genie clucked his tongue. "I'm afraid you can't sleep with housecats here. Millionaires don't do such things. You can have an entire cattery somewhere else in the grounds, with all the Siamese, Persian and marmalades you want."

"But I want Puss!" Verity said.

"Millionaires don't have ordinary housecats," said the genie. "I'm afraid that's definite."

"You can't tell me what to do," said Verity tearfully. "When Mum and Dad get here, they'll decide."

Once again the genie clucked his tongue and shook his head sadly. "I'm afraid your parents won't be joining you here," he said. "After all, they're not millionaires, you know. You can help them out of course. Maybe install them in some more, er..., economical quarters within a few hours' drive. Your chauffer could drive you around whenever you wanted to visit."

"No!" Verity said. "If I can't have my own pony, my own cats, and my own parents, then I don't want to join your old Millionaire's Club!"

She thought she saw a small gleam in the genie's eye, as he said. "I'm afraid it's too late my dear. By this time your application will be nearly processed. Once things are done, they can't be undone, you know."

Verity began to cry. The tears made her vision very blurred, and when she rubbed them dry, she found that she was back in her room. The genie was gone, and Puss was snoring gently. She ran into the lounge, where her father was nodding with sleep in front of the television set. She couldn't restrain herself, and ran and jumped into his lap and held on to him for dear life.

"What happened, dear?" asked her drowsy father. "A bad dream?"

"No," sobbed Verity. "I don't want to join the Millionaire's Club!"

Her father didn't say anything, but her picked her up and carried her back to her room. He laid her on the bed and said, "It'll all be fine in the morning." and went out of the room.

It didn't take but two blinks of Verity's sore eyes before the genie was back. His briefcase was still spinning slowly. She could see that he looked worried.

"Bad news, I'm afraid," he said.

Verity felt another gust of sobs coming on. "That means I have to go now, doesn't it?" She whimpered. "Without Puss and without Mum and Dad and without my room and my garden and without all my..."

"I'm afraid your application for membership has been rejected," he said formally. "I regret to have to inform you that the Board felt that you were already wealthy enough."

And with a sudden twirl of his briefcase, he was gone.

At breakfast the next morning, Verity's mother looked concerned. "Your eyes are all red, dear," she said. "No more staying up reading your pony book by bad light from now on."

But Verity was smiling. She brought the book up from her lap and handed it to her astonished mother.

"That's all right," she said. "I don't need it anymore."

How to Make a Million Pounds

A boy was playing with a toy aeroplane when it sailed into a large tree, snapping one of the propeller blades. He tried to make it fly, but it wouldn't lift off. He took it to his father. "Dad, I need to buy a new propeller for my plane," he said. He was nervous, because he knew that his father hated nothing more than parting with money.

His father frowned. "Do you think I'm made out of money?" he said. He took the toy from his son's hands. "This would cost you at least ten pounds to replace," he said. "Let me show you something."

He took his son into the garage and put the plane on his workbench. Using glue and clamps and two tiny screws, he repaired the propeller. "There," he said, "Good as new."

The boy looked at the propeller. It didn't look as good as new. It looked a little crooked, and the screws stuck out. He was sure it would unbalance the flight of the plane.

"We just saved ten pounds," said his father with satisfaction. "That's ten pounds more we have to spend on other things."

"You mean saving money is the same as earning it? He

asked.

"Yes," said his father, beaming. "Even better."

The aeroplane didn't work as well as before. It flew erratically and the boy had a difficult time keeping it in the air. He also noticed that the propeller looked even more bent than before. The next day he emptied his piggy bank of all he had and went to the shop where the plane came from. The propeller cost £9.99, leaving him with 68p.

A few weeks later it was the boy's father's birthday. His brother and sister brought their presents to the dinner table, where a big chocolate cake with candles on top had been set by their mother. After singing "Happy Birthday" his father began opening his presents. There was a tie clasp from his brother, a book token from his sister and a new Black and Decker drill set from his mother. He opened the boy's present last. It was small, in fact it was no bigger than a card in an envelope, which is what it was. Inside was a note that read, "One million pounds" and 68p in loose change.

His father looked puzzled. "Thank you," he said, turning over the note as if looking for something.

"You're welcome, dad," said the boy. "That's the most I could afford. I didn't buy a private plane this week, and I didn't hire a pilot to fly it for me. I just looked at the pictures instead. Oh yes, and I didn't buy every computer game in the Nintendo catalogue. That added up to exactly £999,999.32 we saved, which, as you said, is better than earning it. Sorry, but I had to make up the difference in cash."

Dozy Rosie

Rosalind was born in the palace, destined one day to become queen. Her parents were delighted at her arrival, as they had tried and tried to produce an heir. She was a rather ordinary looking little girl, but much was made of her, because she represented the future of the kingdom.

As she grew, the whole court waited to see signs of her abilities. After all, she was the offspring of a wise and brave king and his beautiful and talented wife. But as time went on, she showed no particular talents. Her parents hired the best tutors. She was schooled in languages and art and history. She was instructed in horsemanship and archery, but she excelled at none of these.

Rosalind was only really good at one thing: sleeping. She had the ability to pop off into a deep sleep at any moment, whether she was reciting Latin lessons or jumping fences on her large white mare. Privately, her parents began to despair. And behind their backs, the gossips of the kingdom began to call her "Dozy Rosie."

As she grew to adulthood, this tendency grew worse. Apothecaries were summoned to give her stimulants. Mesmerists attempted to overcome her weakness. In desperation, the king instructed seamstresses to create extremely uncomfortable items of clothing to keep her upright at all times. But all this was to no avail. The princess slumbered and the court despaired.

When the day came for her coronation she went to sleep with the newly installed crown on her head, which slipped off and rolled across the marble floor of the court. At the feast, she slept through the last four courses. The whole kingdom was embarrassed, but no one had any ideas.

To make things worse, neighbouring kingdoms were growing increasingly warlike. There had been incursions into the territory of the kingdom, and everybody could sense that war was on the horizon. Advisors wrung their hands, generals fretted, but Rosalind just slept.

A delegation from the hostile neighbour came one day to the palace. They were treated with more deference than usual, because the whole of the kingdom had grown fearful. The Queen was summoned from her bed to greet the visitors, high representatives of state, carrying who knew what fearsome news.

Queen Rosalind was determined to succeed at the conference. She knew all to well how much she carried the hopes of her people. If she could only stay awake, she felt that all would be well.

The ministers of the hostile kingdom were ushered into the court, where Rosalind, dressed regally in ermine and her crown, sat on the throne. This had been made as uncomfortable as possible, in a desperate attempt to keep her awake.

The leader of the hostile visitors wasted no time. "We have come to make certain demands, Your Highness," he said curtly. "Your lands have grown and now include what is rightfully ours. We require immediate restitution, or there will be consequences."

The court gasped. No one had ever dared speak to a sovereign in this way.

"We demand the immediate withdrawal of all your garrisons from the borderlands and the re-drafting of the map of your kingdom."

There was silence. Rosalind had her eyes shut, as if in thought. The leader of the hostile party listened expectantly for her reply, which must be firm and clear. After what seemed an eternity, Queen Rosalind opened her mouth, as if to speak, and gave vent to a single loud snore. Even in this emergency, it seems, she had been unable to remain awake.

All eyes turned to the hostile party. The expression on the leader's face was unreadable, but to everyone's astonishment, he bowed deeply and left the court, followed by his retinue.

A page boy overheard the whispered conversation of the hostile visitors as they hurriedly left the palace.

"If she is no more worried about our demands than that," said the leader, "They must be much better prepared to meet our troops than we thought. We will have to report to our king that an invasion at this time would be unwise." And with that they mounted their horses and were gone.

Dozy Rosie, which is now what their queen was fondly called, slumbered happily for many years thereafter, ruling over a time of peace and prosperity.

Won't Power

A man was beating his donkey in the street. The beast stood still, head down and eyes tightly shut. A passer-by asked him why he was doing this.

"Because he's stubborn and refuses to move," replied the man.

"But don't you know that the donkey is the noblest of all creatures?" asked the other. "Far too noble to be beaten in the street."

"You must be joking," said the man, but he put down his stick and waited expectantly for one of the fool's stories.

"You will remember," said the passer-by, "that Mary was riding on a donkey the day before the first Christmas."

"Of course," said the man. "But that doesn't make him any nobler than a horse or a cat, for that matter."

"Well, this donkey was tied in a small alley outside the

stable behind the inn where Joseph and Mary couldn't find a room. It was a cold night, that first Christmas Eve, and the donkey wouldn't even fit into the stable himself.

"He stood in the alley for days, getting-- like your donkey-- more and more fed up. The food was meagre, there was no roof over his head, and what was worse, he had to shift every time somebody wanted to go into the stable. And there were plenty of visitors. First, a gang of rough-looking types that smelled of sheep. They came and stayed a long time, and when they left, they woke the donkey up.

"Then there were three strange-looking men with camels-- which donkeys, frankly, can't abide. They stayed a long time, too. The donkey had by now decided he'd had enough. He wasn't going to budge to let a single other beast or person past him. He might have to pass his days in a narrow dark little alleyway, but, by goodness, from now on, at least, it would be his alleyway. He wasn't going to shift until he was good and ready."

"And that's noble?" hooted the man. "Why, that's just stubborn, like this beast here." He raised his stick again.

The passer-by continued undeterred.

"The next people who came up the alley were two Roman soldiers. They were, of course, looking for firstborns to slaughter, having been given that job by Herod.

"When they tried to pass the donkey, he placed his whole body across the alley, and just stood there, with his eyes shut. The soldiers beat him and they pushed him. They even poked him with their sharp swords, but they realised, as many a man before us has, that they wouldn't shift that donkey without killing him, which would be a trifle rude and very messy as well.

"And so they went away. This happened because of the donkey's great gift: though many men and beasts have the quality of will power, only the donkey-- in all of creation-- has the gift of won't power. If it hadn't been for that donkey, there'd be no yule logs, no mince pies, and no Christmas."

So you never can tell what bad qualities turn out to be good ones, and how what you're really like can turn out to be holy, too.

Don't Think About a Little White Bear

There was a little boy named Henry who had his very own room. It was a big room in a new house in a new town, where Henry went to a new school. Henry didn't like bedtime, even when his mother came and tucked him in. The new room was very large and very dark.

One night Henry was lying in bed with his eyes open when he saw a little white bear. It was next to his wardrobe, where some clothes were hanging over a chair, but when he looked closely he could see something that looked exactly like a bear. Henry scrunched up his eyes, but didn't quite close them. He watched until—sure enough!—the bear moved.

Henry didn't want the bear to know he had seen him, so he got up very casually and strolled to the door. As soon as he got there, he ran as fast as he could down the stairs and nearly ran into his father, who was coming out of the kitchen.

"What's the matter, Henry?" asked his father.

"I think there's a bear in my room," Henry whimpered.

Henry's father put his hand on Henry's head. "Bears don't live in houses," he said.

"But I SAW him," sniffled Henry. "A little white one with sharp teeth."

"Come along then," said Henry's father. He held Henry's hand and they went back into the bedroom and switched on the light. Henry's father looked around and said, "You see, Henry, no bears here."

"I SAW him," Henry insisted. "Over there in the corner."

Henry's father sat down on the bed and tucked Henry in. "Let me tell you what to do," he said. "Just don't think about the bear. If you don't think about it, he'll go away." He gave Henry a kiss and went out, switching off the light.

Henry lay awake for a long time trying not to think about the little white bear. He kept his eyes shut tight, but every once in a while he peeked. And every time, the bear was still there.

In the morning Henry was tired. He was sleepy at the breakfast table and just wanted to go back to bed. His parents talked in low voices and his mother gave him an extra kiss. Henry didn't notice, because the little white bear was trying to get into the kitchen with them. He could see him out of the corner of his eye, but he remembered what his father had said and tried not to think about it. But on the way to school, Henry saw him twice, once hiding in the shrubbery and once behind the bus shelter.

All day Henry tried not to think about the bear. This was difficult because he spotted him hiding behind the teacher's desk and then he was waiting in the corridor at three-thirty when school was over.

His mother asked him about school but he didn't answer. He was too busy not thinking about the bear. She clucked and gave him an extra biscuit.

That night Henry fell asleep on the sofa and his father carried him upstairs and put him in bed. As he switched out the light, Henry woke up. He was fed up with not thinking about the bear. So he looked in the corner of the room and saw the bear moving around in the dark. Henry just watched. It felt good not to try to forget about him. The bear came out and looked back at Henry. He was all white, from head to tail. He had large teeth, very pointy ears and a shiny black nose. He stood still looking at Henry until Henry said, in the bravest voice he could manage, "What do you want?"

The bear scratched his head and came over to the foot of the bed.

"I want to dance," he said.

So Henry got up and danced with the bear. Then they played a game of hide and seek and a game of tag. They stood on their heads until one of them fell down first, and then they laughed until morning.

When Henry got to the breakfast table the next morning, he still looked tired. Who wouldn't be tired if they danced and played with a little white bear all night? His father looked at him a long time, like fathers do when they don't understand something. At last he said, "You're not thinking about that bear again, are you?" he asked.

Henry got up. So did the bear, who had been sitting at the table across from him. Maybe he could get the bear to carry his books to school.

"Bear?" said Henry, "What bear?"

The Day God Popped Round

There was an old man who had everything he could ask for. A nice little house where he lived alone, a garden full of good things to eat and a very nice view from his window. But even so, this old man wasn't happy, because-- though he had seen many things-- he had never seen God.

One night he fell asleep and he dreamed a dream. In this dream there was an angel who told him, "Look, Old Timer, your wish is going to come true. Tomorrow God will pop round for a visit."

The old man woke up very excited. He got up before dawn and mopped the floor, ironed the curtains, and mopped the floor again. He washed the dishes and shined the silver and washed the dishes again. By breakfast time he was sitting on the front step, looking eagerly out at the road for a glimpse of God. About nine o'clock a figure appeared in the lane. The old man's heart raced, until he saw that it was only his neighbour, wanting to come in for a chat.

"Not today, friend," said the old man, and the neighbour went away.

The morning wore on and turned into afternoon. Again the old man saw a figure approaching down the lane and leapt to his feet. Once again he was disappointed, because it was only his daughter bringing him one of her sweet berry pies. He sent her away in a hurry.

The day trickled away and the shadows got long in the lane. In the gloom the old man saw another figure approaching. "At last!" he exclaimed, jumping to his feet. Then his heart fell, because he saw, not God at all, but only the town drunk, weaving his way toward the house in hope of a last drink before going home. The old man spoke to him sharply and sent him scurrying away into the dark.

The whole day had passed, and God had not come. In despair and fatigue, the old man dropped down on his bed and fell instantly asleep.

And dreamed a dream. In this dream he saw the very same angel. The old man shouted at him, "I thought you said God was coming here today!"

The angel inspected his fingernails and replied, "God asked me to tell you that he tried three times to visit you, but each time, you sent him away."

Then, after a long silence, he smiled and said, "But he'll probably be back tomorrow."

Heard told by Rev Michael Joyce